Acknowledgements

Thank you to my family, I will love you all until the end of time. You are the air that I breathe. To my friends, thanks for keeping me afloat when I thought I would sink. To my cover model, Redd Lauren, thanks for doing your thing on the photos. You rock everyday! To my fans and many followers, I love you all more and more each day. Thank you for the love and support you deliver each day!

To book Bianca Daniels (Redd Lauren) for cover modeling contact biancaldaniels@gmail.com or www.thicktoppmodels.webs.com

DEDICATION

I would like to dedicate this book to my family and my friends who supported my dream of becoming a published writer. They believed in me when I didn't believe in myself years ago. I'm making you proud now! Also to my readers for without you there would be no me. I love you all!

To some very special readers who have been rocking with me and supporting me from day one, I love you all. This book goes out to Latosha Scruggs, Jackie Figueroa, Yung-Lit, Tiffany Haynes, Camille Lamb, Nefertaria Ayo, Fallon Willis Blaqk, Keyanna Savage, Shemika Jones, Sharon Blount, Courtney Bryant, Keona Day, LaShaun Cadney, Rosalyn Reed, Shanta Shaw, Me'Tova Hollingsworth, LaSonya Steger, Lakenya Ross, Candice Preyer, Tiffany Williams, Nae Martinez, Shikira Hoy, Tona McCoy, Shamella Skipper, Linda Jiggets, Marissa Palmer, Tonia "First" Maurice, Sistar Tea, Sandy Sims, Carla Towns,

Brandie Davis, Joy Hammond Nelson and Tanisha-PhatPhat. I'd also like to dedicate this book to the Facebook Book Clubs that support me, New Beginnings Book Club, RRU, We Read Urban, Just Read, SRS, Slyce, Tajana Sutton's Club, MUB, KR, Bayou Diva Readers, and last but certainly not least The Nicety Readers!!! Love you all!

Thanks to Tamika Newhouse & AAMBC for their support and my award for Break Out Author of the Year for my novel Juicy: Pandora's Box!

Special Shout outs to #TEAMNICETY, the bullets to my nine!

To my besties…you all know who you are as I will only use first names but your love and support knows no bounds. Mario, Guillermo, Ashley H., Ashley P., and Ashley P. (Yes I meant to do that), Jeanne, Yvette, Bob, Manny "You're so silly", Arndell, Leslie, Princess, Walt, Will, Karen, Theresa, Tiffany K., Irine, Meron, Earline and Jermika. I want to thank you from the bottom of my heart for always supporting me and making sure that

I remained focused on the task at hand, which was getting your books to you on time. Laughing but dead serious. To my husband, the perfect verse over a tight beat. Thanks for being nothing more than you!

If I have forgotten anyone, know that I love you still

"Sleep is for people who don't work hard enough" — Nicety

Chapter 1
Picked Up

"What the fuck?" Messiah snapped as he reached for the gun from Bentley's hand one second too late.

Federal Agent Crosby was stretched out on the concrete with a single gunshot wound to his dome, set perfectly between his eyes. They were glossed over and were still open from the trauma of it all. All the while, the warm summer wind blew his cheap looking toupee to the side revealing a semi bald head. Red froze with her hand covering her mouth in disbelief that Bentley had actually shot a cop. She thought his whole scene was all just for show, a simple scare tactic. Messiah tried to calm his boiling point before he was able to assess the situation.

"I'm sorry, Meech. I'm so sorry to do this at your place of business." Bentley covered his mouth in horror at the amount of blood oozing from the detective's head.

"Sorry ain't gon' scrape this nigga's shit off the ground and keep the heat off my business. Is it?" Messiah retorted angrily.

"Well I'm out. I see you're busy with this shit so—" Red began to walk away but was interrupted by the tight grip of a hand on her arm.

"No! You ain't going no where." Messiah grabbed her arm forcefully. "Don't even think about walking away."

Red snatched her arm away from his grip then crossed them sending him a funky look. She rolled her eyes and stood there but she couldn't bring herself to look into his eyes. He knew she was still angry with him but he was determined to make her listen to what he had to say. He just couldn't deal with her right then but couldn't bear to watch her leave.

"Skid, get Danger and get up here. Some shit just went down." Messiah hung up his cell phone and stuffed it back inside his pocket.

Danger and Skid reached the storage opening with Braze tagging along behind them and the shock on their eyes read like braille. They looked at Bentley standing there with an expression of guilt on his face and immediately became angered by it. Neither of them were in the mood to clean up his dirty work since it was bad enough that they had to clean up the stiff downstairs. Messiah rubbed his head wildly, feeling his blood pressure skyrocketing.

"Alright, I need y'all to clean up this shit here first before that shit downstairs. I can't have this out here when customers get here man so I need this done now." Messiah demanded.

With that, he reached up pointing the gun blasting two slugs into Bentley's chest. His body made a loud thud sound as it hit the ground with everyone's eyes focused in on him. Messiah lowered his hand looking down at his body without an ounce of remorse flowing through him. He motioned for the guys to take care of him as well.

"Scrape that dumb ass up too. Shit." Messiah spat handing the gun to his brother.

"Dude what the fuck is going on? Man Meech, I'm telling you shit is getting too crazy out here, dog. This shit ain't as tight as it used to be, man. You got enough money. You need to retire." Danger said placing his hand on his brother's shoulder.

"Why? So you can take over and run the shit into the fucking ground for real. Look, I give the orders around here, alright? I got shit to do. Make sure this shit is handled before the doors open." Messiah retorted as he placed his hand on the small of Red's back escorting her to his truck. "That's your job."

Braze shook her head at his anger trying to fix her lips to respond but was interrupted as she looked down at the wet goo dripping down her legs. She didn't know how long it had been there but realized it was definitely time. There wasn't any pain as of yet and she could not even feel the baby move. It wasn't the time or the place to be going into labor but it seemed she would not have a choice in the matter now.

"Meech!" Braze shouted rolling her eyes at Red. "I'm in labor."

"Oh no. We ain't playing that shit again." Skid said wrapping the final piece of blue tarp around Agent Crosby's dead body then helping Danger toss it into the back of his truck's trunk.

"No really! I'm in labor. Look!" Braze said pointing down to the sticky residue soaking her jogging pants.

Messiah looked into Red's irritated eyes and knew his talk with her was going to have to wait just a bit longer. He signaled for Braze to get in the truck and watched as the look on Red's face went from angry to pissed. Braze hopped her ass conveniently in the front seat leaving Red to lackadaisically take the back.

The guys were pouring bleach on the ground attempting to clean it up and watched as Messiah backed out of there speedily.

"So what we gon' do with these motherfucking bodies man?" Danger snapped, pissed that now he had to burn his brand new Sean Jean fit.

"Shit. We gon' do what we used to do back in the day, take 'em to the Stew Maker." Skid replied checking the ground for any leftover residue.

"Damn, I didn't know that son of a bitch was still in business." Danger smirked.

"Yeah, and the sooner we get these stiffs in the truck, the quicker we get rid of 'em. So move your ass." Skid replied grabbing the second blue tarp from out of a box and tossing it to him.

Danger laid the tarp down right next to Bentley's body and with Skid's help, rolled him onto it. Gurgling, moaning sounds filled their ears as they looked down realizing that Bentley was still alive. Skid didn't want to waste anymore time out in the open with bullet-ridden bodies. He wrapped the tarp around his body securing it tightly then signaled for Danger to aid him lifting it.

"Alright. You clean up the blood and I'm gon' get this bitch from downstairs." Skid said as he headed for the elevator.

Danger was pissed. He hated doing the dirty work. As Skid loaded onto the elevator, Amy waddled off examining the scene her man was cleaning. She noticed the angry look on his face and knew she shouldn't ruffle his feathers about leaving her downstairs with a bloody corpse for so long. She placed her hands on her hips releasing a deep sigh before looking up into his eyes to speak.

"Babe, what the fuck happened up here?" She asked in a soothing voice.

"Man, motherfuckas trippin'. That's all. Why didn't you stay downstairs?" He responded angrily.

"You left me down there with a dead body in the fucking dark and shit. You got me fucked up, goofy." Amy retorted.

"Girl, I'm up here handling business. You can't help me with this being pregnant and all." Danger curled the bottom of his t-shirt around his fist, using it to clear the droplets of sweat from his forehead. "Maybe you should take the car and gon' on home."

"Uh un, you know I'm not leaving you."

"Amy, I'm good girl. All the drama is over. You need to give our sunshine some rest. She had enough excitement for one night."

"Boy you don't even know if its a girl or not. Them doctors don't be knowing shit til the baby come out. Fuck those ultrasounds. Your ass just want a daughter that damn bad."

"You right I do but not if she's gonna be as hardheaded as you. Go home, Amy!"

Amy didn't have time to rebut his demand as the elevator doors opened up. Skid stepped out dragging Zadie's heavy carcass in a dirty blue tarp. He made his way to the truck holding the other two bodies and with Danger's help loaded the final body into it. Skid slammed the fly door down ensuring it was locked and secured tightly before making his way over to close the storage door. He tapped the keypad turning on the alarm then headed over to assess the cleanup effort.

"You did a good job there, boy. Ain't shit left on that ground. Shit, you'd make a good house nigga." Skid joked as he slapped the back of Danger's shoulder.

"Man shut the fuck up man and get yo' big Shaq lookin' ass in the damn truck dude." Danger snapped pushing him back. "Look babe, just go home."

"No. I ain't fucking going nowhere." Amy curled her lips and crossed her arms.

She was adamant on going with him. She got clingy like that with every job that they did ever since she got pregnant. Danger hated it but he knew she was only smothering him because she was nesting. He didn't want her to meet the Stew Maker. There were things in that place that even the most ruthless vathos had never seen and he was afraid she might be traumatized by it all.

"Babe, where we going isn't a place for pregnant women—"

"D. you can talk that shit all you want but I'm going and that's that." Amy walked off, jumping in the back seat of the truck.

Honk! Honk! The horn annoyed him and interrupted his thoughts. Skid was an asshole like that, not wanting to wait on anything when it was on his time. He looked over to the driver's side mirror seeing his eyes mean mugging back at him. He rubbed his head as he headed for the front passenger seat and jumped in. *Damn.* Danger thought as he wished like hell he could persuade Amy to get her stubborn ass out the truck before they pulled out the gate.

It was too late. Skid had already tapped the button on the sun visor and exited the gate as it slid open. As they drove along the road and eventually merged onto the Stevenson Expressway, Danger began to relax about bringing Amy along. She was a beast, after all, and could damn well handle herself in any condition. He realized he might have been tripping over nothing. Skid blasted the Mrs. Officer by Lil' Wayne allowing it to penetrate the speakers from the radio station. Amy sat still in her seat unfazed by the fact that not one foot from her was the bodies of three dead people, one of which was a cop.

Once off the expressway they drove a few blocks then pulled into the back alley of a commercial neighborhood. Amy didn't journey to the North Side much but she knew that's where they were because the buildings were much taller and the streets were much cleaner than any other parts of the city. She knew they had to be about to fuck with someone of great prestige since only people with money lived in that part of town. Even the alleys were clean like no one ever even threw a single piece of gum or potato chip wrapper on the ground.

"Wait here."

Skid parked just before a long black gate with a tall wooden fence covered behind it, so no one could peek in. He exited the truck, heading up to the gate appearing as if he was whispering something into the gate. Danger and Amy sat in the car and watched as the gate opened giving a soft buzzing sound as it did. Skid reentered the truck, revving it up as he maneuvered it backing it into the grassless yard instead of pulling straight into it. The three flat building behind them was all brown brick with no visible stairs and the windows were all covered with newspaper on the inside.

"Skid, where the hell you got us at, dude? This is an abandoned building with a dusty, dirty ass yard and shit." Amy wondered, looking puzzled at the yard's dead like appearance.

"Ay, shut the fuck up, alright? When we go in here don't say shit cause you liable to get cut. Alright?" He retorted slamming the truck door.

"Nigga, how the fuck we supposed to get these stiffs out the trunk without motherfuckas seeing this shit in broad fucking daylight?" Danger panicked.

"You worried about shit that don't concern you. Let's go." Skid said signaling him to follow.

They headed for a set of concrete stairs in the back of the building leading down to the basement. The door swung open automatically with a guy standing there holding an AK-47 guarding it. He escorted them deep into the back of the dark dungeon past long hanging chains with hooks attached to them. They could hear a loud buzzing, rattling sound in the distance that was slowly becoming more apparent the closer they got to it. Amy tried to remain calm, making sure to focus in on her surroundings using her other senses since her visual was more than obstructed by darkness. The only light visible was the light from the guard's cigarette lighter that he held up for them.

"In there." He said pointing to a room with light illuminating all around the edges of the door.

The man disappeared into the darkness leaving them there to fend for themselves in the dark. There was no going back, as Skid walked up to the door, pushing it open. The revving sound was slapping them in the face but it was drowned out by the display before them. Amy felt sick to her stomach feeling as if she would barf right there on the cold concrete floor. The only thing helping her to hold it back was Skid's words before they walked in the building.

She placed her hand gently over her stomach while her baby did back flips inside.

"Stew Maker, respect from Big Meech. We request your services." Skid said in his most humble voice.

"How many?" The Stew Maker asked very sternly turning the chainsaw in her hand off.

"Tres." Skid responded.

"Who are they?" The thick accented Mexican female asked.

"Familia."

She removed the huge black rubber gloves from her hands and the matching ski mask from her face. Long dark hair flowed from her head dangling all the way down her back and just above her muscular plumped backside. She wore extra thick makeup around her eyes and dark deep black lipstick. Her dark colored jumpsuit was very tight fitting almost spandex like with all black leather Timberlands adorning her feet. The woman didn't smile and it seemed like she didn't blink as she hawked Danger and Amy down, studying them like an AIDS test.

"Familia, eh? Okay, thirty large." She spat placing her hand on her small hips.

"Thirty large?"

"Ten a piece, motherfucka you got a problem with that?" She snapped curling her eyebrows over something wicked.

Skid put his hands up. He knew he wasn't in the right place to be trying to negotiate deals. All of them looked over at the dripping half a corpse hanging from the chains over a huge dirt hole in the ground. There was only an arm and leg left on the torso with the genitals still hanging out from it.

Blood was splattered everywhere. On the opposite side of the room, there was a huge pot about the size of a MACK truck's tire. It was sitting atop of a gas fire with the lid being heated by burning charcoal. It was very unusual to them that the pot wasn't giving off any foul aroma or stench. Instead it smelled like they were in a fast food restaurant waiting on their order. Turning back to the woman impatiently waiting on an answer about her money and a dead hanging corpse made them realize this was no fucking restaurant.

"Well, thirty large or what, huh?" She said walking up to them.

"Yeah…yeah no problem." Skid responded.

"Huuugh." Amy placed her hand over her mouth to stifle her vomit.

"What's wrong with this one, eh?" The woman pointed angrily.

Danger grabbed her shoulders and pulled her back hoping Amy didn't let one drop of it touch the floor. "No, no. It's okay. She's just pregnant."

"Hmph. I need the cash now then." The woman demanded walking over to the table radioing in to someone on her walkie-talkie. "Get them."

Danger's ears bled when she said that. He was wondering what she meant by "them". They hadn't done anything wrong and had sealed the deal so he couldn't understand why she was betraying them. Skid stood there shaking his head at Danger and Amy knowing she had no business coming there with them. It sickened him that he couldn't keep his broad in check. He turned back to the woman as she placed her ski mask back over her head and slipped her massive gloves back over her small hands.

She revved up the chainsaw once more forcing Danger and Amy to jump back in terror.

"Mover! Mover!" Two men walked in yelling in Spanish ordering them to move out of the way as they brought in one of the bodies and tossed it on the ground like it was nothing.

The Stew Maker went back to work on her current victim without another word uttered to them. Skid knew the drill with her and signaled for Danger and Amy to get the fuck up and out of there. They quickly moved towards the back exit passing the next transport of carcass and were relieved to see daylight again. They made it to the car with one body left for the men to remove.

"Hey! Hey! Dinero, bro!" One of the masked men said knocking on the driver's side window with the AK in his hand.

"Oh yeah." Skid said reaching into his glove compartment and snatching out three of the five neatly wrapped stacks inside. "Here ya go."

The man flicked his thumb across the paper loving the sound it made as it slapped together. He nodded his head and bounced to the back of the truck helping his counterpart remove the last body from the back. The guard at the gate waited until the men were inside and shut their door before he opened the gate for them to leave.

"Hey, güey. You might wanna close your fucking trunk, eh." The guard laughed as they exited the yard slowly while he slammed the trunk door down for them.

"Ay, yeah, bro. Thanks." Skid waved back peeling out like a bat out of hell as he wiped droplets of sweat from his forehead. "Shit them Mexican Cartel motherfuckas ain't shit to fuck with."

Chapter 2
Oh Baby

"Agh! Aggghhh!" Braze screamed at the top of her lungs.

She really wasn't in pain at all but she figured she would need to keep up appearances. Not only was it working but also she was commanding all of Messiah's attention, which had her grinning from ear to ear inside. Braze rubbed her protruding belly with one hand and caressed his arm with the other. Her constant sounds of agony distracted him from anything else she was doing as he struggled to drown out everything in order to speed past cars unscathed.

"Oh, Braze. Don't you think you may be over reacting just a bit bitch?" Red snapped rolling her eyes and folding her arms.

"When you go into labor then you will be able to talk to me about overreacting. Otherwise just shut the fuck...up, please." Braze countered lifting her head to yell towards the back seat.

"Ok, I'm gonna need the both of you to shut the fuck up since I am the one weaving in and out of traffic, here." Messiah bellowed raising his hand up halting the argument.

They finally pulled up in the Emergency driveway of Christ Hospital. It was the closest to the Candy Shop. They all exited the car with Messiah carefully securing Braze's arm in his hand, escorting her as she waddled into the sliding glass doors. Red followed close behind disgusted by her very presence.

It was hard for her to just let what she did go simply because she was pregnant and in labor. She had no remorse or sympathy for her whatsoever.

"Ma'am. Ma'am, she's in labor. Can you help us?" Messiah asked helping her into a wheel chair that one of the orderlies immediately scooted towards them.

"Okay, sir. We are going to admit her and start a drip but while we do that I'm going to need you to fill out some papers for me. Okay?" The nurse said handing him a pen and a clipboard with thick set of papers attached.

"Uh…what?" He stared down at the papers like they adorned foreign words upon them. "Ma'am, I don't think I should be doing this."

"Aren't you her husband?"

"What? God no!" Red replied snatching the papers out of the nurse's hands.

The very short and thin Asian nurse hawked at Red like she had the plague but quickly turned her attention towards her new patient. Her coworker had already begun Braze's IV and left to prep a doctor on her condition. The nurse tucked her cropped cut hair behind both of her ears then leaned in to check her vitals. Once they checked out, she went to grab a fetal monitor to hook up to her belly.

"I'm writing your name on all of these papers, just to let you know." Red said crossing her legs as she scratched on the paper.

"I don't care. This hospital knows me very well anyway." Messiah replied.

"Oh yeah that's right. Isn't your fucking wife upstairs somewhere?"

Messiah sighed heavily. He didn't like for her to speak about Alexis since it only aroused resentment within him and anger within her. Even though it pained him to think about what he had done to Alexis, he still couldn't shake his love for Red. She was his no matter what and there was no way in hell he would allow her to walk out of his life because of his whore of a wife. The guilt of what he had done and his vows were the only think still bounding him to Alexis, though, but he knew Red wouldn't wait forever. He was torn between doing the right thing and loving the right person, which seemed to affect him more now then ever seeing that Braze was having his baby.

"Yeah...she's up there." He replied in a low solemn voice.

"Wow..." Red mumbled as she completed the paper work, slamming it down on her lap.

Braze watched from a few seats down as Messiah and Red gazed at each other lovingly. It made her sick to her stomach watching the spectacle as if they were actually a couple. Her lips were as dry as sand as she licked them hoping to relieve the crusty feeling they were giving. She ruffled her ponytail trying to clean herself up to look more presentable for Messiah. The more she looked over at them the more vomit rose in the back of her throat.

"Huuuuuugh!" Braze released pinkish brown chunks onto the floor.

The feeling was no longer just a mere thought, it was reality. Braze wiped her mouth with the back of her hand as a fleet of nurses rushed over to her aid. Messiah sat there with his head hanging down pissed that he was in this predicament. He couldn't bring his self to show his care for her with Red sitting right next to him. He was weak for her and it showed.

"I'm going to need to move her to a room right now!" The head nurse yelled to her subordinates.

"What's wrong with her?" Messiah bellowed above the crowd.

"Yes, what's wrong with me?" Braze asked worriedly.

"The baby's vitals aren't showing up on the monitor and you are shading pale. The baby may be in distress so we need to go in right away." The nurse replied helping the staff load her onto the gurney. "Alright people let's move!"

"Wait I need to go!" Messiah yelled as he moved with the crowd.

"No sir. She needs you here. When we've calmed everything down we will send for you." One of the staff nurse's stopped, pushing him back as they continued to hurriedly wheel Braze out of sight.

"Damn!" He exhaled beating his fist against the counter.

"Come on, baby. She'll be all right. They'll take good care of her." Red reassured him as she caressed his broad back.

Her touch sent chills throughout his body. He turned wanting to embrace her soft caress but as he gazed into her eyes he knew it was neither the time nor place. The buzzing sound in his pocket interrupted their sweet solstice stare, pissing him off once again. It was hard for him to ignore it this last time, since it had been going off for some time now, seemingly back to back. He eyed down at the caller ID realizing that he had about thirty missed calls from the morning alone. As he scrolled through the log, it buzzed wildly again.

"Yes!" He said turning away, making sure not to yell in Red's face.

"Uh, yes Mr. Torres?"

"Who is this?"

"Mr. Torres, I've called to tell you the status of your wife's condition. I thought you'd might like to know that your wife, she's awake sir."

Messiah paused breathing heavily into the phone. His soul damn near fell through his feet and on to Hell as he pressed the phone even closer to his ear. It was as if he were dreaming the doctor's words but he knew he had heard them loud and clear.

"Sir?"

"Yes…I'm here. I'll be there shortly." Messiah replied hanging up quickly before anything else could be uttered.

"Who was that?" Red crossed her arms as he turned staring deeply into her big beautiful brown eyes.

"The doctor."

"Are you really going to make me dig for information here, baby?" She said side eyeing him.

"Alexis…she's…she's awake." He sighed holding his head high as if to show no weakness.

"Ah, now that wasn't so hard to say now was it? Well, aren't you going to go see her? I mean, you're right here." Red spat.

"I don't have time for this right now. I have to check on Braze and the baby." He said walking over towards the desk.

"No, Braze and the baby will be fine. Let's go see how wifey's doing." Red smiled.

"Huh? You wanna go?"

"Of course baby. I'm just a concerned employee. Remember, Meech?" Sarcasm rang through her voice.

"Eh, baby maybe you should stay here. I'm going to run up there real quick and see was crackin' then I'll be right back. Okay? Just stay here." He said grabbing her hips trying to convince her not to move.

"Oh no baby. I'm going with you. You ain't that slick." Red smiled fiddling with his short goatee. "But nice try."

He was convinced of one thing, that she would go up to the room and start some bullshit with his weak wife. He wasn't prepared to go through that but he knew once he snapped back at Red she would surely leave and possibly disappear off the face of the Earth. He didn't want to leap any bounds trying to track her down when he could just keep her right by his side. He swallowed the lump in his throat and took her by the hand shooting her a sly smile.

"Alright, baby doll. We'll play it your way." He said leading her towards the elevator.

It was a response she wasn't prepared for. She knew he would fight her to the death to remain behind. She hadn't anticipated that he would be willing to do anything to keep her including out his love for her in front of his ailing wife. The elevator dinged and opened allowing them to step on. Messiah pushed the button for the 4th floor then stuck his hand in his pocket as the doors closed. Every minute of the ride made Red's stomach flutter. She felt that since she had never even laid an eye on Alexis this would be one hell of a way to do it.

They exited the elevator. Messiah seemed to be taking extra large steps in his shiny patent leather shoes. Her small frame struggled to keep up as he squeezed tightly to her hand, sweaty palms and all. He would prove to her once and for all that you truly get what you ask for. He walked right up to the big glass paned room door, room 425. He stared at it hesitant but knew it was now or never. Red stared up at him wondering what he was waiting for. He reached out for the handle and walked in.

"Wait." Red said pulling him back and roughly yanking his arm. "I can't do this. I'm sorry. I…I just can't right now."

It was almost a dollar short but it came right on time in his eyes. "I understand. Wait right here. I won't be long."

He smiled at her gently kissing the top of her head then headed in the room. It seemed that whole moment Red was holding her breath wondering if she would pass out before they got to the room but she never did. She couldn't bring herself to boldly walk into the woman's hospital room and make her presence known like that. It was rude, and tacky, and just plain ridiculous in her mind. If Alexis would find out about his love for her it wouldn't be on her sick bed and it wouldn't be from her. It was his duty to tell her what was going on between them. *He'd fucking better.* She thought. *When she's well enough to handle it.*

But curiosity did kill her sweet little cat as she died to know what kind of woman she was. She was intrigued by the thought of her, this woman who once held his heart bound so tightly. She had to know what she looked like, how she carried herself, and what they were like together. She needed to know how she wore her hair, moved her lips, and batted her eyes. Red slowly walked over to the door peeking around cautiously to see if she could catch a small glimpse of her face. Even if she could see nothing but her skin color she just needed to know something about her. Her eyes caught her face turning to him as he walked over to sit beside her. His body blocked her view as she bobbed her head to get around him. And then he moved. Red's eyes widened as wide as the sea as she covered her mouth releasing a slight gasp.

Chapter 3
There Goes My Baby

"Argh!!!!" Braze screamed out in complete and utter anguish.

She gripped the side of the bed clenching the sheets in between her fingers strongly. Her eyes focused on the pink scrubs that the small Asian nurse who brought her into the room was wearing. It was a pretty soothing color to her eyes and helped her to concentrate on something other than the excruciating pain penetrating through her belly. The pain kicked in tenfold once they found out the baby was in distress. She lay back on the table praying for some sort of relief.

"Ok, Braze we are going to give you some pain medicine in your IV. You can't get an epidural because we need to find out what's wrong with the baby first." The nurse said sticking a needle in the skinny tube hanging from the drip bag.

"What? What's wrong with my baby?" Braze asked.

"We don't exactly know yet but we are about to find out." The white-coated doctor interrupted.

"What do you mean you don't know exactly? Doc, don't let my baby die! Don't let my baby die!" Braze cried allowing both of her hands to swallow her face.

"Just calm down. We're going to do all that we can. Okay?" The doctor responded nonchalantly.

His tone did not soothe Braze's sobbing. She didn't feel like she could trust him. He gave off a distasteful persona that she didn't care for one bit. She prayed like hell that Messiah would come bursting through the door, wrap his big bulky arms around her and assure her that everything would be okay. The clock on the wall above the under lit baby cleaning table, displayed the time but no matter how hard she squinted the numbers remained blurry.

"Someone call my baby's daddy. Please!" She shouted from the top of her lungs with tears flowing freely from her reddened eyes.

The nurse shook her head in disgust at the young girl who obviously was focused on nothing but her man. A nurse prepped her for the doctor's examination but Braze's screams only made them not want to touch her. The small nurse walked out of the room allowing the other nurses and doctor to continuously hook her up to machines and exam her.

"Alright ma'am. You're just going to feel a slight tug and pinch but nothing major. I just need to manually see if the baby is choking from the cord." The doctor said as he reached his hand down digging deep inside of Braze's opening. "We need to get this baby out now. Okay prepare for delivery." He signaled to one of the nurses.

"Please just tell me what's going on!" Braze cried out, her face drenched in tears.

"Braze, I'm going to need you to take a deep breath and push okay. Whenever you feel a contraction just push into the pain, like you're taking a dump." The doctor responded.

Something inside of her knew that whatever was going on with her she would never find out until the very end. She knew something was wrong with the baby but they were hiding it from her for some reason. If they were trying not to stress her out they were doing a horrible job. Braze pushed with all of her might as sweat droplets dripped from her forehead. She released an angry torrent from her dry cracked lips as she gripped the side metal bed rails. The nurses locked her feet into the stirrups so she could not move and all the while she could only wonder where the hell was Messiah. Braze huffed and puffed repeatedly, anticipating the next contraction.

"Can someone find my fucking baby's daddy please?" Braze begged loudly to the orderlies again. "Aghhhhh!"

"Ma'am, someone is going to find your kid's dad okay? Just calm down and focus on getting your baby out safe." The doctor requested sternly.
****

Red couldn't believe what her eyes were seeing. She instantly remembered where she had seen Alexis' face before and it shocked her to no end. The last time she had seen Alexis she was walking out of her apartment with Danger following close behind.

"Baby, I missed you so much. The only person I could think to ask for was you." Alexis smiled rubbing Messiah's forearm seductively.

"Alexis, let's not act like we haven't been having problems. I mean, I'm glad that you are alright and all but we can't put on this front." He said slowly removing his arm from her tantalizing touch.

"Having problems? What kind of problems baby? Whatever I did I'm so sorry but you are my husband and I love you." Alexis replied with worry in her eyes.

"Huh? You mean you don't...awe damn." Messiah lowered his head in disbelief.

"I don't remember much but I remember you babe. Just marrying the greatest guy in the world. I love you. Whatever happened between us we can fix it." She pleaded with him caressing the underbelly of his chin.

"Uh, I need to go talk to the doctor real quick. I'll be right back."

"Okay babe. I'll be here. I love you."

"Yeah...yeah, give me a second."

Messiah walked out of the hospital room noticing Red as she dipped back around the corner on the outside of the door. In the hall he looked for the attending physician who had been taking care of Alexis since the accident. He was leaning against the counter writing in a big white folder full of papers and adjusting his wide round glasses at the same time. He didn't even notice Messiah walking up to him.

"Hey man. You neglected to tell me that she had amnesia."

"Well, you didn't give me time to and you said you be right here so I figured I'd tell you in person. Uh, how did you find out anyway?" The doctor asked bewildered.

"Because I just came from out of the room talking to her and she wasn't herself."

"Ah yes...and she won't be. Not until her memory is jogged enough to bring back everything she lost."

"Ugh, doc! So how long will this take?"

"Mr. Torres this is not something you can readily place a time factor on. It could take months, maybe even years before she gets her memory back. It all depends upon what she remembers. The brain is a fickle thing."

"Years? Doc, I don't have years. Hell, I don't even have months, okay? I need her back to her old self like yesterday." Messiah said feeling his blood pressure rise.

"I'm sorry, I don't know what to tell you. Now if you'll excuse me, I have other patients to tend to."

The doctor's cold treatment skyrocketed Messiah's boiling point times ten. He didn't want the brush off he wanted answers but it didn't seem like he was going to get any from him. In his mind, there had to be some kind of way to get her memory back and fast. Alexis was not normally that pleasant and loving but he knew that if he left her in her weakened state he would be more than the monster he already was for causing the whole mess. He lowered his head using his index finger and thumb to caress the shaft of his nose to relieve the tension forming in it. A firm hand on his shoulder interrupted his thought process.

"You okay?" Red asked warmly, concerned that the bit of news he had just received wasn't good.

"Yeah. I'll be good." Messiah grabbed her hand from his shoulder giving it a slight peck. "Com' on. Let's go check on the baby."

"Sir! Oh my gosh, I've been looking for you everywhere. Your wife is requesting your presence in labor and delivery but I must warn you that the baby is in distress." The Asian nurse bumped square into Messiah's shoulder headfirst.

"She's not my wife." He replied.

"Ugh, to tell you the truth sir I could care less. But the patient is asking for you so please, follow me."

They followed the nurse hastily back down to the room holding Braze. Messiah never let go of Red's hand making sure she was by his side every step of the way. They ran down the stairs and to the second floor all the way to Braze's delivery room hand in hand. The nurse turned to a cart sitting in the corner next to the room handing Messiah a pair of gloves and a facemask.

"You might need these." She said throwing them in his hands nonchalantly. "But she can't come."

"Wait!" Messiah watched as the nurse disappeared into the room. "Damn, she ain't even trying to hear me. I ain't even get a chance to ask her if you could come."

"It's okay. I ain't really wanna go in there anyway. Go on. Go see your son."

"You sure?" Messiah asked checking for a disappointed expression on her face.

"Yeah. Shit, you gotta see your first born come into the world." Red walked away and copped a squat on the bench a few feet away.

"Yeah…yeah I guess I do." He replied slipping on the blue linen gloves and mask he was holding. "Alright. I'll be right back."

Red shook her head as he jetted into the room. All that could be heard was Braze's agony that eroded from behind the door. She could feel the pain she was in with every screech she made. It was if she was in labor herself. She placed her head in her hands and kneeled down to her knees wondering what the hell she was even doing there. She knew Messiah had too much going on in his life to ever fit her into it but his persistence drew her in. She had to admit it turned her on to have him clenching to her every move.

Her head began pounding like a hammer to a nail as she looked at the clock posted on the wall above her head. She had been sitting there for over an hour but had just not realized that the excruciating screaming had stopped more than ten minutes ago. The room door didn't have a window on it like the ones upstairs so she couldn't peek through to see what was happening. It was eerily quiet in the hall and she began to wonder why Messiah hadn't ran out of the room in celebratory praise of the birth of his newborn son. She stood pacing the floor in front of the door determined to grind a hole into the ground until he came out. There were voices on the other side of the door but she couldn't make out whose they were.

"Oh excuse me." The doctor said as he bumped into her. He exited the room with three of the nurses following behind him.

She peeked her head around looking in the small slit of opening in the door before it closed. The door closed so fast she was unable to see anything. Red sighed and plopped back down on the bench, slouching and biting her nails off their hinges. She had almost scratched a hole in her head before the door came flying open and out came a somber looking Messiah. Before he could speak she was up out of her seat and in his face. She didn't know whether to curse him out for seemingly forgetting about the fact that she was out there or ask him what was wrong.

"Is everything good with the baby?" She asked hesitantly realizing he didn't need bullshit in his ear right then.

"The baby." Messiah paused.

"Oh baby. I'm so sorry honey." Red said as she clung to his broad shoulders.

"I think I'm going to call him MJ." Messiah looked up glaring in her eyes grinning from ear to ear.

"Huh? So he's alive?"

"Of course he's alive. He's a healthy strong baby boy. Messiah junior, but to me he'll be MJ. He's so beautiful, Red. I can't wait for you to see him."

"Oh…yeah." She felt guilty that a part of her felt disappointed. "I mean that's great baby! Congratulations!"

"Thanks. That's my boy! My baby boy!"

The gleam in his eye was one of a very proud father. She hadn't seen a look so bright since the days when her father used to look into her eyes as a little girl. She wrapped her thick arms around his neck hugging him tightly as he kissed her neck and squeezed her waist. Red would support him and show him just that. There was no way she would take that moment away from him by asking him to get a blood test for the baby. Even though he was sure the baby was his, she knew it would not hurt for him to be sure. After all, Braze was an evil conniving bitch who would stop at nothing to have him all to her self and the thought never left her mind no matter what state she was in.

Chapter 4
"You Stupid Bitch!"-- Danger

"Alright you motherfuckas better have y'all stories straight if motherfuckas come 'round asking about shit. You know what I'm saying?" Skid said as he pulled up in front of Danger's truck parked in front of the shop.

"Yeah, we was at the crib 'til she went into false labor and we just not getting back. I ain't seen you or nobody else. We out." Danger replied solemnly.

He slammed his car door and escorted Amy to their truck parked right outside of the Candy Shop gate. They didn't speak a word to each other as they drove on headed back towards their house. Nothing needed to be said since they were both already thinking the same thing. The shit their eyes had just witnessed just a short while ago was one for the books. All of the contract hits they had performed didn't prepare them for the shit at the Stew Maker's den.

"You aight baby?" Danger asked as he pulled up in front of their pad and turned the key to the ignition.

"Yeah. Shit I guess I'm gonna have to be right?" She said staring straight out of the front windshield unable to blink.

"I told you to go home man. You so hardheaded." He caressed her bobbed cut blonde hair.

"Dude, you knew I wasn't gonna let you go that easy. We in this shit together right? We are a family and we gonna ride as one."

"Shit, in a minute you 'bout to hang up your guns and butter to be a stay at home mom. I ain't 'bout to have my baby momma out here putting herself in danger and shit."

"Man, are you crazy? What about you? You risk your life every got damn day. What we gonna do without you? What is your baby gonna do without a daddy?"

"He or she would have their momma who would hold it down for them. Amy, its one thing to lose me but kids can't live without their mommas babe. Trust me, I know." Danger snapped scratching his head and lightly beating his fist against the steering wheel. "Fuck me. You gotta live for the baby."

"Danger, I can't stop being me just because I'm pregnant and a momma now. I'm a killer. That's what I do." Amy sighed heavily. "Don't make me choose between my career and my family."

Amy turned allowing him to gaze into her big blue sparkling eyes. He loved the way she stared back at him and could never resist it. It was one of the main reasons he fell in love with her in the first place. Her face exposed the grimmest look but he wasn't about to let her intimidate him with that. He meant what he said and he didn't give a damn if she agreed or not. She fought him on working while she was pregnant and he gave in, but this was the one time that he was standing as a man and putting his foot down.

"Making you choose would be giving you an option and I don't remember making an offer." He said removing the keys from the ignition and exiting the car.

"Hey how the fuck are you just going to walk off like that? We were fucking talking." She howled exiting the car, slamming the door behind her and getting in his face.

"I was done talking, Amy. You are not carrying on with this business and that's final. You need to start thinking like a mother."

"I am thinking like a mother. I pull in more money doing that than sitting on my ass. I don't know how to do shit else 'cause I've been doing this shit since my dad taught me at fucking thirteen years old, Danger."

"Well, you've got three months to find you something else to do because you ain't doing this. Now I'm done."

Amy stood there in the middle of the sidewalk heated from their discussion. He wasn't trying to hear her talk more bullshit in his ear. He walked up the stairs of their two-flat building and turned the key to the outer wooden glass paned door. Amy refused to walk in the house behind him as pissed as she was and refused to look in his direction as well. She stared off into the distance at the niggas posted outside of the corner liquor store on 79th and Escanaba.

It wasn't unlikely for niggas to congregate there early in the morning. It was their dip off spot to sell their dope and the store owners allowed it as long as they vowed to protect their store from whack ass robbers. She squinted her eyes as one dark clothed man moved throughout the crowd. He seemed to slither through shaking the hands of some of the men out there but never skipping a beat.

"D. D." Amy's whispers fell on deaf ears. "Danger...Nicholas!" She got his attention then.

"What the hell you want calling my government all out like that? Is you crazy?" Danger said opening up the door.

"Danger, I think I see Pet."

"Who? Where?"

"Right there baby. He's crossing the street now." Amy nodded speaking through her teeth and trying not to seem obvious.

Danger peeked his head around passing and parked cars and through the walking pedestrians to catch a peek. He didn't know if he was looking at the right person and truth be told he really couldn't see far away that well. He patted Amy on the shoulder signaling her to follow him in the house. She stood there with her eyes fixated on the man walking away from them drifting further and further into the distance.

"No, babe. That's him. That's fucking him right there." She was adamant. "I think we should go get him right now."

"Woman, you don't even know if that's really him. He's all the way down 79th now and the sun is probably just playing tricks on your damn eyes." Danger brushed her off.

"Damn it. It wasn't the sun! I saw him. He was right there and now he's turned the corner and gone. You let him get away."

"Man I'm not about to go up to know strange dude thinking that's him and it ain't then I look like the fool. Com' on woman, let's go in the house." He said grabbing her by the hand. "Besides, that nigga probably long gone by now. I know he ain't that stupid to stay in the hood after that shit he did to Red."

"You don't think he's that stupid huh? Well what if he is? If a person is crazy enough they don't give a shit about that kind of shit." She replied as she walked in the house behind him disappointed that he didn't believe her.

"Babe, it's okay. That fool gon' get what's coming to him soon enough. In the meantime we got some make up sex to tend to."

"Excuse me? Oh no don't think you're off the hook that quick. I'm still pissed at you, D."

"Well you can be pissed with this dick in your mouth, baby." Danger threw his cell on the glass coffee table and plopped down on the big black microfiber suede couch unbuttoning his jeans.

"Oh you want these jaws wrapped around your long, thick black dick huh?" Amy crossed her arms and shot him a sly look and smirk.

"Shit, hell yeah baby!" Danger beamed stroking his beef making sure to get it nice and firm. "You know how I like it? What you waiting for?"

"For you to realize that I'm never gonna be your prim and proper housewife. I'm just not gonna be able to do it babe."

"Amy, got damn it! You fucking up a good moment bringing this shit back up, now. Why can't you just drop this shit?"

"Because you are trying to strip away apart of me. This is who I am, this is who you fell in love with and this is the only thing I love to do."

"So you want me to believe that you love to kill motherfuckas, Amy?"

"Yes...I do."

"You know what, whatever. 'Cause after you see that precious bundle of joy you ain't gonna be thinking about shit else but that."

"What? Danger, are you even listening to anything that I am saying to you?"

"You just haven't started really getting your nesting on yet. As soon as you start that I'm sure you will fall right into motherhood."

One thing was very clear to her; he was as much in denial about the true nature of their relationship as she was. They had no idea who each other were. They had been together for four years having met at the Candy Shop when she was a regular bagging girl and he was security. She upgraded to one of the killers when Messiah saw how she handled a nigga who tried to steal from him. She and Danger have been together ever since but now she was beginning to realize that all they had in common was killing niggas in cold blood, sex, and the precious life growing inside of her stomach. The more they disagreed on her position after the baby was born the more she began to believe that the creature cultivating in her womb was more of an abomination than anything.

"Danger, we have problems in this relationship. You don't know me and I clearly don't know you."

"Awe, here we go. What you want now? Huh? You wanna go shopping, is that it?" Danger said still blowing off the issue.

"No! I want you to acknowledge me and my feelings in this relationship. I put up with your shit way too long not to be getting treated fairly and now I'm carrying your fucking child and all I keep thinking is that this is a mistake!"

"Amy you are just tired from all the bullshit of the night and you need to eat and sleep. That's all that's wrong with you."

"Ugh. You're not listening! I don't want to be some housewife or stay at home mom. I don't want a man who doesn't respect my decisions or dreams or one who can't keep his dick in his fucking pants and I definitely don't want this baby!" Amy snapped. "I mean it ain't like I got no fucking rings on my finger or nothing."

Her words tore a whole in Danger's face as huge as the ozone layer. She stood there calming her breathing realizing what had just flew out of her mouth but she wasn't sorry. He wasn't supposed to find out that way but he had pushed her to it. There was a dead silence in the room but she could hear his breathing like he was right up on her ear. His facial expression remained still and solemn, which made it difficult to read what he was thinking. She proceeded to walk off wanting to be done with the discussion now that the truth was all out in the open. Her feet hit the stairs ready to head up to their bedroom to pack her things. She needed to separate from him for a while, just to clear her head.

"You stupid bitch!" Danger had pounced on her like a lion to a cheetah turning her around on the stairwell and choking the living daylights out of her. "Is that what this is about? Huh? A ring? You wanna get married…huh?"

His fingers dug into her neck creating a long lasting print and trembling like crazy. Drool dripped from his mouth as Amy stared into his buck-opened eyes scratching at his hands hoping to pry them off of her. She kicked while trying to scream but only being able to let out faint choking noises and droplets of water from her eyes. Her heart fluttered a mile a minute and consciousness was quickly fading from her being. He saw her giving up and slowly relinquishing her body unto his. Tears flowed from his eyes as he realized what he was doing but the rage that was buried inside of him blew out in an instance. In his mind, it was uncontrollable.

Chapter 5
Getting Haggled

Skid sat at his elongated wooden dining room table with a short glass and a fifth of Scotch. All the shit he had ever seen throughout his career as a killer and he had never seen anything like the shit the Stew Maker did. He was sickened by the fact that someone could do something so vile to a body and still be able to sleep at night. He was more of the shoot 'em up and leave 'em stankin' type. But because Bentley killed a cop he knew it had to be done. As he took a sip of his drink, the erratic knocking that overwhelmed his door startled him.

"Who the fuck is it?" He yelled, words slurred from drunkenness.

"Mr. Talbert, it's the Chicago Police. Open up man I don't wanna have to break down, now." An officer yelled from the other side.

He recognized that voice from anywhere but he never thought he'd hear it again. It had been a whole entire year since he was released from parole but every now and again when something went wrong his old officer, Haggley, harassed him for information. Skid, being an old timer to the streets, he figured he always had the connect on what was happening. But even if he did, Skid didn't like to participate much. He wasn't a snitch and even if he was he hated the fucking police.

"Man, what the fuck you want Haggley? I ain't did shit and you ain't got no fucking warrant, so leave me the fuck alone." Skid answered rubbing his face trying to straighten his self.

"Awe, you know better than that. Open up, let's go."

"Man, fuck man." Skid snapped as his muscular arms turned the top bolt lock then the bottom door lock before opening the door. "The fuck you want, man."

Haggley looked around the room noticing that Skid was very neat and clean for an old bachelor. He walked over to the dining table that was adjacent from his large black leather sofa and took the glass Skid was using. He sniffed its contents then chuckled a bit as he placed it back down, returning it to its resting position. He glanced over into his kitchen and over towards his bedroom area of the studio apartment making sure the coast was clear before he spoke any further.

"So, I see we are back on the wagon again huh?" Haggley smirked.

"Man, what the fuck do you want? I ain't did shit." Skid snapped plopping down on the sofa hoping to fall asleep and cut the officer's visit short.

"No, you probably didn't do anything, but I'm certain you know who did."

"Man, I don't even know what you talking about." Skid replied folding his arms and getting cozy.

"Let me tell you a little story. One day I was walking down the street and heard some the streets talking. They told me you weren't making that much money out here. Got your panties all in a bunch for chicken change. Now I, myself, couldn't stand to hear that. So I decided to pay my ol' pal a visit."

"And you come here all the time yipping that bullshit in my ear looking for something to eat and every time I tell you my motherfucking refrigerator is bare you don't seem to get it. Why do you come here? You know your ass is out, man. You need to be puttin' your ass to the streets as in working. Fuck outta here, man, with that 1980's Ed McMahon suit on. You don't run me no more." Skid waved him off.

"I thought you might feel that way. That's why this time I decided to extend a little offering, you know, man to man."

"What?" Skid looked over confusingly. "What kind of fucking offer?"

"First I need the body of my buddy, Officer Crosby. I know he's dead so don't patronize me and I know your buddy Messiah is behind it. Secondly, I need Messiah, alive. And in return I'll give you $1.5 million dollars."

Skid sat straight up staring Haggley dead in his eyes searching for a hint of bullshit in them. In all the times he came snooping for evidence or information he had never offered up anything let alone cash money. He was wondering why he decided to come to him in the first place figuring like he might already know something. But he played it cool knowing there was no way he could link the dead cop's disappearance to him or Messiah's business.

"You see his partner reported him missing last night when he saw that he left some vital things behind that he normally wouldn't. He didn't take his car and he didn't tell anyone where he was going. But we suspect that maybe he was going off to do some work on his own." Haggley said snatching some playing cards off of the mantel next to the front door. "Now his family done bumped the arrest money up to a half a million dollars and that would look real nice in my nest egg.

"What's that got to do with me?"

"We know that he was investigating the Candy Shop. Crosby was keeping a watchful eye on your boy for a reason. Your boy Messiah has a hefty bounty on his head and just like me he was trying to be the first to get at it. As his right hand man I'm sure you know about the debt he done racked up with the Italians up north. Tsk, tsk, tsk, it's not looking good for ya boy! So all I need you to do is call me when you've got the body and your boy, together. Call me only! No one else! Just me. Is that cool?"

"Meech is legit man. He don't do no bullshit up in there—"

"Hey man!" Haggley roared quickly. "This is some real shit."

"Aye, man. How the fuck I know it's real? You talkin' bout throwing me a million dollars and shit. I'm sayin' how the fuck you gonna give me that kind of dough on a hood cop's salary?"

"Maybe I'm not your ordinary *hood* cop. Look, I know for a fact that you know something about this. Bring me the missing cop and your boy and you get paid enough cash to disappear and never have to worry about me again." Haggley smirked as he headed for the door. "Serve them up, asap."

Haggley walked out of the door with a smug look as if he had won Skid over and feeling like he was big shit. He knew that kind of money would entice him to get up off of his ass to get him what he was looking for. Skid sat on the sofa pissed that Haggley always came to him for every little piece of bullshit he needed help with. Messiah was his man, a hundred grand, so the thought of betraying him in some shit like that had never crossed his mind. Until today. That money would definitely put him into retirement for good and send him under a rock where no one could find him.

The only problem was the fact that he couldn't exactly give Haggley what he wanted. Since his trip to the Stew Maker, he was unable to deliver the body of agent Crosby to him. The Stew maker very rarely kept any parts left over, being sure that she was as thorough as possible with clean up and everything. Besides anyone who stepped in her territory unannounced was fucked, period. He also had to think of how he would explain what happened to Crosby without implementing his self or Messiah so he could still get the money and bounce. Haggley didn't give him a time frame and that was the only good thing he could think of at that point. It gave him enough time to figure some shit out.

"Yeah." Skid said as he took his cell out of his pocket, punched the talk button hard then placed it half way up to his ear.

"Yeah, that business is taken care of?"

"No doubt." Skid replied walking to the table pouring another shot of Scotch.

"Good. I'mma need you to go open up the shop. We ain't got nobody to do it and I know you at the complex so you ain't shit but up the street."

"Man...I really wasn't trying to do that shit Meech. You can't get your bro to do it? His ass ain't on shit."

"Yeah and his ass ain't answer the phone neither. Naw, I need somebody who I know is gone handle business. It's just for today. Tomorrow, I'll put Red up there til I hire somebody."

"Com' on Meech, dude. Really?"

"Yeah, really. Business needs to resume as usual. No question."

Messiah hung up the phone without waiting for another one of Skid's whinny responses. He needed the Candy Shop open for business like nothing had took place there that morning or the night before. No one could be suspicious as to the abrupt unexpected closing of the joint and even if they were closed customers still had access to the place to be able to access their units. He needed to make sure that nothing was out of place or looked suspect, making sure that it looked as normal as it did before blood hit the pavement.

He stuffed his phone back down in his pocket. "Com' on baby. I need you to do something for me."

"What is it?" Red asked following him as he grabbed her hand in his.

"I need you to go hold down the fort for me while I get a few things squared away."

"Huh? What fort? The Candy Shop? Oh naw dude you got me messed up if you think I'm about to sit up there and do nothing all day."

"I'm paying you though."

"Are you serious right now Messiah?"

"I know. But I need you right now. Skid is going to be there so you won't be alone. But I need you, Red. You're the only one who's down for me and who I know will hold down the fort 'til I get there." Messiah sighed. "So what'll you say? Will you hold ya boy down for a little while?"

Messiah turned on the puppy dog eyes and gazed deep into hers. She wanted to slap the taste out of his mouth for even fixing his lips to say something like that. She was trying to be stuck to his hip like glue now that both his wife and his baby's momma would summon him any chance they got. They were two bitches not to be trusted and she wasn't about to let Messiah slip back into guilty love with either of them. Even though Red was still burning mad at his ass, she knew deep inside of her she wanted him. She needed him.

"You owe me, so big!" Red snapped rolling her eyes.

"More than you know. Thanks babes."

"Yeah, yeah. Let's just get out of here before I change my mind."

In the truck, Red wanted to ask him about the conversation that he had with Alexis so badly. She itched to know what he told her and how she took the news. *Messiah wouldn't let me down, I know it.* She thought as she gazed out the window shifting her mind over to MJ. In retrospect, she really couldn't be mad about the baby. He was conceived before she came back into the picture but apart of her couldn't help but wonder what it would be like if he was hers. Up until the time her feelings had sparked for Messiah, the thought of settling down and having kids with anyone hadn't crossed her mind at all.

"I can't believe I have a son now." Messiah blurted happily, unconscious of his words.

"Yeah."

"He's so big. I can't wait to hold him again. Man, it's the greatest feeling in the world." Messiah wasn't even thinking about how all of this affected Red.

"Okay. I'm just gonna go ahead and say what you're not supposed to say. Are you sure it's yours?" She snarled.

"What? How could you ask me something like th— Of course he's mine."

"Don't get defensive, I'm just saying. There could be a possibility and I know you know that. I mean you were fucking her sister for God sakes. Don't tell me it never crossed your mind." Red turned to make sure he hadn't shut down on her.

"Yeah. It's crossed my mind. But when I saw his eyes they just reminded me of old pictures of myself when I was little. You're right though. I'll think about it some more." Messiah replied solemnly.

The car was silent the rest of the way to the shop. Red was relieved that she had at least resurfaced the idea in his head about getting a paternity test done on the baby but she felt a little bad that she had blown the high he was on about being father. He wasn't cheery or talkative anymore he had shut down. When he pulled up in front of the shop Skid was standing outside of the office door smoking a cigarette.

"Ay, gimmie a kiss." She said before placing her hand on the door.

Messiah locked his lips with hers rotating and massaging his tongue with hers. The kiss was so soft and delicate that it sent vibrations right down to her v-like opening.

"Mmm. I swear you owe me." Red smiled as she exited the truck.

"Yeah…I know." He responded after she was already out.

He nodded towards Skid as he backed out of the parking lot and swerved back into traffic. His mind ran a marathon trying to figure out his next move. That doctor needed to give him more answers than what he did as he headed back to the hospital in haste.

Chapter 6
Amy Cracks

"You done lost your mind talking about you don't want my fucking baby! Are you crazy?" Danger squeezed her neck tighter and tighter.

Amy gasped for air digging her nails into his hands hoping to scar him enough to release her. Tears began to form in her eyes and slowly drip down the sides of her cheeks. Her throat was so compressed that she couldn't even plead with him to stop. As her face turned a bluish green, the thought set in that she was about to die. He was trying to squeeze the very life out of her regardless of the baby she carried in her womb. Then Amy dropped to the floor abruptly, coughing wildly and holding her neck.

"Don't you ever say no shit like that again! You hear me?" Danger snapped. "Now you staying your ass here with the fucking baby and I don't wanna hear shit else about it. I'm gonna let Meech know too, so you won't have any work to do. Suck on that."

"You stupid motherfucka." Amy cried and snarled in a raspy voice. "All the shit I done took from you, all the bitches…and this is how you do me? You don't even want to fucking marry me but you want me to be your fucking housewife."

"Damn! You bitches always want a nigga to marry your ass but you ain't willing to do what the fuck we tell you to do. Don't no nigga want no disobedient wife."

"FUCK YOU! I've stuck by your ass through all the hoes and all the sleepless nights! The Gonorrhea! Obey you, motherfucka respect me!"

"I was going to make you my wife, when the time was right Amy."

"I'm seven months pregnant, Nicholas. When will it ever be the right time, baby?" Amy responded tranquilly.

"Man…I'm out. We talk about this later. Why don't you fix yourself up and shit. We need to calm down." Danger replied before walking out the door.

Amy sat there with tears flowing carelessly from her eyes. She had heard stories from Danger's past about him putting his hands on his other females but in the time that they had been together he had never put his hands on her. In some twisted way she thought he respected her more than that. Her heart was beyond crushed having never experienced anything like that from any man she had been with. No one ever got to the point where they needed to put their hands on her no matter how slick her mouth became.

Amy picked herself up off the floor clenching her stomach. She could feel the baby readjust itself inside of her womb as she grabbed a hair tie to pin her long blonde hair into a low ponytail. Unable to stop her tears, she reached for her phone wanting to talk to him and make it right but ended up tossing it across the room. She didn't want to work it out with him, not this time. This time was the last straw with her. As bad as she wanted someone to talk to she realized he wasn't the one. An orphan of the state she never knew her parents or any other extended family members and friends weren't wise to have in the field of work she was in. Sometimes friends got smoked too.

"You wanna fuck with me, knowing what I'm capable of? Then I'm gonna hit you where it hurts." Amy spat to herself as she walked out of the room.

She went downstairs to the kitchen and grabbed a bottle of Whipped Cream flavor Smirnoff out of the fridge, leaving the glass behind. Danger had been saving that bottle for them to enjoy after a candlelight dinner once the baby was born but she figured why wait. Her fingers quickly popped open the top and placed the opening of the bottle to her lips breathing in the sweet smell of the liquor. Amy licked her lips loving the smell rising up in her nose having not had a drink in six months since she found out she was pregnant. It was as if she hesitated for a minute, staring up at the ceiling awaiting the cool clear liquid to flow into her mouth and down her throat. It felt like heaven.

"Stupid motherfucka." She ranted as she walked back towards the stairwell. "You don't own me. I do what I want. If I want to have a drink I'm just gonna have drink. I don't need you!"

She went on and on like that for a few minutes pacing back and forth from the kitchen to the hallway checking the window, making sure his car hadn't pulled out front. She took another swig of the drink before rushing to the sink to pour the rest down the drain. It was only a matter of time before he noticed it was gone so she disposed of the rest of the evidence and shoved the bottle deep down into the trashcan. He wouldn't see the bottle through the black trash bag.

"Now, I feel better. The only person who cares about me is me. I'm not about to listen to you anymore. I have to live for me." Amy mumbled drunkenly as she walked back towards the window to catch one more glance before heading up to bed.

She grabbed the curtain peeling it back slowly but was interrupted by the sound of Sex Ain't Better Than Love reverberating through her cell phone. There was only one person who was assigned to that ringtone and she was amazed that he had decided to call. Usually when they had fights he would just storm off and not come back home until 3am unless he forgot something. But the fact that he called wanting to talk spoke volume. Amy hurriedly stomped the stairs rushing to the bedroom. She grabbed the phone but as soon as she pressed the button he had hung up.

"FUCK!" She barked raising her fists in the air waving erratically.

Amy's anger rose higher than the clouds, staring down into her cell screen hoping that Danger would call back. She prayed over the phone yearning for him to call and beg her to forgive him and promise do right by her from now on without any restrictions on what she can do after the baby is born. In the middle of her prayer, Trey Songz interrupted again and this time her finger was already on the trigger.

"Hello?"

"Yeah, Amy, what you doing?

"Is that why you called me?"

"No. I just needed to know if you got that AK that I sat on the dining room table. I'm gonna need you to put that up for me. I'll take it to The Candy Shop tomorrow since I know how much you hate the pieces being in the house."

"Is…is that the only reason why you called me?" She asked in a soft feeble voice.

"Uh, yeah. Did I need to say something else?"

She couldn't believe it. She was practically giving him an out to the argument. The buzz of alcohol was running through her bloodstream so warm and thick that the initial look of shock or disbelieve became stuck on her face but wouldn't allow her to cry. Her finger loosened allowing the cell to drop through her hand and onto the floor. Vomit rose in the back of her throat and flew out of her mouth as she grew dizzy and clasping her stomach and falling to the floor. Her knee slipped on the top stair sending her body plummeting down the staircase pumping her head, back and protruding stomach along the way.

"Argh!" She bellowed from the bottom as she attempted to get up. "Help!"

Amy looked around realizing she was the only one there and struggled to get up again. Her body was completely sore from the fall making it difficult for her to determine which of her limbs, if any, were broken. She screamed out in agony as she rose to her feet examining her body. Wiggling her arms, fingers and legs it appeared that she was going to be able to walk away from this accident unscathed. She limped over to the couch and took a seat relieved that everything was okay.

Squish. As soon as she sat down she felt gooey ickiness on her ass cheeks. She slipped her hands in between her legs to investigate the gush she had sat in wondering was it already on the couch before she took the seat. When she raised her hand back up, the bloody wetness dripping down her hand shocked her. Amy panicked rising from the couch slowly to find her phone and call an ambulance. She could feel the blood rushing out of her like a waterfall now and immediately knew something was terribly wrong with the life inside of her.

"Oh my God…Oh my God!" Amy spat shaking trying to steady her fingers to dial 911.

"Amy! Where you at girl?" Danger yelled as he walked in the door slamming it behind him. "You still on that bullshit?"

"I'm right here. Baby, something's wrong." Amy replied quietly with tears in her eyes and her mouth opened wide.

"What…what's wrong with you?" Danger asked as he walked into the room.

Amy gradually raised her hand in the air showing him the excessive amount of blood on her hand as he walked up the stairs towards her. He slowed his movements almost in disbelief that this was happening. She began to cry hysterically knowing that she had fucked up royally, feeling incapable of telling him. She knew if she told him that he would go ballistic and she would get much worse than the choking she had received earlier.

"What the fuck is happening?" Danger asked worriedly. "Come on let's go…now!"

Danger grabbed her hand almost dragging her down the stairs to the front door.

"Wait! I can't go that fast, Danger!"

"You gotta try alright? We gotta make sure the baby is okay."

"I know but you're hurting me!" Amy cried holding her arm underneath her stomach. "You're dragging me!"

"You gotta get to the hospital now!" Danger snapped unlocking the car door, shoving her in quickly. "My baby can't die like this. Oh shit! I'm sorry, Amy. I'm so sorry!"

"Just drive. It'll be okay."

"No it won't. I shouldn't have choked you that badly. I shouldn't have…I can't forgive myself if this baby dies because of me, man."

"You? Oh, baby—"

"Look when you get to the hospital just don't tell them I choked you. I'm sorry and I promise to never put my hands on you again." Danger said grabbing her hand interlocking their fingers together.

Amy's ears burned from his words. She wasn't stupid or naïve and wondered why he often thought she was, talking to her as if she would buy his bullshit. She knew he was lying and would fuck her up easily the next chance he got since the door was open to it now. She side eyed him as they drove on pulling into the South Shore Hospital parking lot while his cell phone rang at the same time. He ignored it.

"Sir. Excuse me sir. Can I help you?" A nurse asked flagging Danger down before he ran past her bursting through the surgery doors.

"Yeah, my girl needs a doctor. She bleedin' and shit man, something's wrong with our fucking baby!"

"Ok calm down sir. I need to get everything straight. Now what happened?"

"She…I don't know just something happened. Fucking help her man! Fucking help her!" Danger was hysterical.

"D. calm down baby." Amy pleaded clenching her belly in excruciating pain.

"Sir, I am going to help her but you need to calm down." The nurse replied calmly signaling for the other nurses to come and help her with their new patient.

They scooped Amy up into a wheel chair and hauled her off through the back double doors of the emergency room. She looked back staring into Danger's eyes. They were sending a secret message between the both of them that neither of them could decode with their words. As the dark skinned chunky nurse pushed papers in Danger's face for him to fill out while he waited until he was able to go back there with Amy, his cell buzzed out of control.

"Yeah, what up joe? I can't talk right now man I got a fucking emergency."

"What's da deal?" Messiah asked.

"Nothing, just gotta see what's wrong with the baby, man."

"Aight handle ya business. Hit me back."

"Yep."

Chapter 7
Skid & Red

"Ugh. Are you just going to sit there and look crazy all damn day or are you going to talk to pass the time away?" Red said throwing her feet up on the counter pissed at the fact that she was even there.

"Yep."

"Damn, would it kill you to join the human race and interact for a change, Skid?"

"Listen, I don't even know why I'm here. Tired of babysitting grown motherfuckas in this bitch."

"What are you trippin' for? I mean it ain't like we working hard in this motherfucka or something. Don't nobody come up in here unless they trying to rent a unit and shit for the most part everybody that comes here just opens the gate, handle their business, and leaves. You trippin'." Red laughed as she picked at her nails realizing she was due for a touch-up.

"No. I'm talking about babysitting you motherfuckas. Like I'm y'all daddy or some shit. Y'all grown. I should be out in the street doin' real shit, big shit." Skid slumped over in the chair stomping his feet on the floor, planting them.

"Hmph. I thought you were doing real shit. Excuse the fuck out of me."

Skid side eyed Red then shook his head. She had no clue that she was never going to be able to replace Messiah's one true love and he knew it. He wanted to snap on her and burst her bubble but her knew it wasn't his place. Besides she would eventually get her feelings trampled on once Alexis got out of the hospital. It was only a matter of time before the cloud she was riding dissolved from under her sending her plummeting to the ground face first. Instead, Skid sighed heavily and folded his arms trying to keep his composure, focusing on the conversation he had earlier that day.

"Fine. Sit there in silence all damn day. See if I care." Red rolled her eyes and began fiddling with the computer trying to find music to play.

"Ugh. Alright. What do you wanna talk about?"

"Ah. I knew you'd see it my way. Well maybe you could tell me more about, oh I don't know, Alexis."

"What? Man, look you ain't about to have me sitting here pillow talking with your ass. You wanna know that man's business then ask his ass. Alright?"

"Yeah. Damn, my bad." Red said flicking her long dark hair behind her ear. "It's just I've never met her and with all the commotion that's been going on I haven't really had time to talk to Messiah."

Skid looked over at her pitiful beautiful face and couldn't help but feel his heart pump for her. He was soft for women in distress and even though deep down inside he knew she was playing him he couldn't help but to give her an answer she.

"Aight, if that nigga asks we never spoke of this."

"No problem, Skid. I would never — "

"Don't fuck with me, okay? Just keep your mouth shut." Skid said opening the compact refrigerator under the desk pulling out and orange Crush soda. "When Meech met Alexis I knew she was going to get his ass. She pretended to be this good girl going to college for law and shit. But really she was a gold digging ho who only saw dollar signs when she got with him."

"And he couldn't see through her bullshit?"

"Man, she had that nigga's nose wide the fuck open. I tried to tell him at one point but I guess I waited too late to do it."

"Why'd you say that?"

"Cause by the time I got a chance to talk to him he was already gone. Nigga said he was in love and shit and about to propose to the bitch and shit. He had never talked about no female like that. I don't know there was just something about her." Skid took a gulp of his soda.

"Has…has he ever talked about me?" Red asked lightly, almost not wanting the answer.

"Briefly."

"Are you really gonna make me ask, Skid?"

"He just said that he used to babysit you and can't believe how great you turned out. Up until the time you popped up out of thin air, he's never said anything about you. Alexis was all he could think about."

Red had to admit that the truth stung a bit. She figured he never stopped thinking about her and his love was undeniably strong for her. Even if it could have been, Skid only confirmed her worst fear, which was that his wife had a hold on him. Her task now was to find out how much of a hold and if it could be broken. One thing was for sure she was tired of being put on the back burner and played because he was torn between them.

"Look, I'm gonna be honest with you, Red. If you looking for that nigga to leave that bitch when she gets better, you crazy. He'll never do it. She's like a leech that you just can't peel of your skin then all of a sudden you find your blood all drained out and then you die."

"He's stressed though. If he was happy he wouldn't be trying to get with me."

"Yeah true. I mean he fucked with them other bitches on some fucking shit cause it was hurt by all the niggas she fucked with on him including his own brother."

"What? Oh my God, no he didn't."

"Yes he did and still was up until the car crash. Meech knew the whole time. He had me follow her every time she left the house late at night to find out the new ones she was banging. He kept count, fourteen." Skid chuckled and shook his head.

"Wow! But we haven't had sex yet so that means he really cares about me. I'm not like those other bitches, not like Braze or Zadie."

"Ah, yeah. Zadie, that bitch was a beast. Damn shame. But Braze, well she's got something you don't have. I'm not sure how he feels about locking her down but he was soft on her, no doubt."

"Soft huh? Well I ain't worried about that. Low level bitches like that are no competition to me. Wait, what does she have that I don't have?"

Skid looked over at her with a raised eyebrow. He knew she had to have known but she was playing the stupid card right then. The awkward silence filled the air as she stared into his eyes truly awaiting an answer. She had apparently forgotten all about where she had just came from and the morning's events. Her patience grew thin waiting on him to answer her as she began to curl her lip up at him.

"What?" Red blurted.

"Are you that damn naïve or are you stupid?"

"Okay we were just doing fine but you ain't about to start disrespecting me calling me names and shit."

"Red, the one thing she has that you don't have." Skid said rocking his arms back and forth in a carriage motion.

"Oh my God…" Red gasped realizing she was in fact being stupid. "The baby."

"Bingo!"

"Shit. I totally forgot about the little bastard. Anyway we don't know if that baby's really his. I mean, she's a hoe, she could've easily had gotten pregnant by anyone of you fools at the shop…right?"

"I don't know, Red" Skid shrugged. "But what I do know is that she was a virgin according to Zadie. She was mad that Messiah got to her cause she knew Braze would be like a helpless puppy for him. Especially when she got pregnant. That's all I'm saying." Skid said finishing off his soda and shooting it into the trash can cross the room as if he were in the NBA playoffs.

"A virgin? That scandalous bitch told that lie. Braze looks like anything but." Red tried to assure herself.

Skid chuckled some more as he shook his head in disbelief at how naïve she truly was. Though she was young minded, he did believe that she had what it took to get what she wanted out of Messiah. It fascinated him how he got all of those young bitches on his dick like that and mostly attracted the ones that could easily get gone in the head. Skid looked down at his cell, gasping silently once he saw the number. He stuffed it back in his pocket determined not to answer it but the moment that it stopped it started back up again.

"Aye, I'm gonna step outside for a minute." He said to Red slapping his hand on the counter playfully.

"Aight." She replied still lost deep in her thoughts.

Skid's phone sang again. "Yeah." He answered.

"Ah, Mr. Alvin Johnson." Haggley replied.

Skid didn't recognize the number but he knew who it was by the way he said his name. Only dicks called him by his government like that and accentuated every letter in it just to piss him off. He didn't want to talk to him but he knew if he hung up it would be nothing but bullshit started. Sweat droplets fell from his face. Skid wiped them away blaming it on the hot, end of June sun beating on his pores but deep inside he knew better.

"The fuck you want man." Skid replied displeased.

"Now is that any kind of way to talk to the man who is about to make you filthy stinking rich?" Haggley answered.

"Man, speak on it man."

"I just called to find out how you were looking on that demonstration." Haggley voice became stern and serious.

"Dude, I told you I don't know nothing."

"Ha ha ha. I'm sure you don't. Well keep your ear to the streets. I will be in touch."

"Look man. I don't know what you're looking for him for but maybe he don't wanna be found. Did you ever think of that?" Skid snapped into the phone.

"Don't fuck with me, Mr. Johnson. I could make life for you a living hell and you know that. I suggest you play ball with me on this one homeboy. You don't know the kind of people that are involved here." Haggley threatened.

"What the fuck? Why me?"

"Cause you're the only nigga in the mix with that fool that could bring him down clean. I don't need no problems in this and you are the right hand man, right? Then do your fucking job and get the work in. I don't give a fuck how you do it, just do it. Got it?" With that, the rest of the conversation was a dial tone. Skid shoved the phone back down in his pocket angrily.

"Fuck!" He bellowed wishing the day's events had never occurred.

He was stuck between a rock and a hard place not knowing which way to go. It was something he wasn't prepared to think about at the moment wishing he had never answered the damn phone. Skid walked back inside the office trying to shield the disheveled look on his face from Red. He didn't want her questioning him about what was wrong. He wiped his face and exhaled deeply as he took his seat back behind on the side of the counter.

"So, who doesn't want to be found?" Red said bopping her head to the beat of Lil' Wayne's Mrs. Officer blasting through the computer speakers.

"Nobody."

"Why are you so guarded, Skid?"

"Why are you so nosey, Red?"

"Because sometimes people need to be pushed to get things off their chest. You look like you need somebody to talk to."

"Why you actin' like you care? You playin' Captain Save-A-Nigga now?"

"No. I just know how if feels to be alone and not have anybody to listen to your problems and fully understand them. That's all." Red spat looking down at her flip-flops remembering the days when she was homeless on the cold streets of Chicago. "Everybody needs somebody."

"Yeah well I don't need nobody. I've been on my own this long, taking care of myself and being my own best friend. So no, I don't need nobody to talk to. Thank you." Skid retorted folding his arms and staring blankly out of the glass door.

"It's still nice to have that option though. So just to let you know, whenever you need to, I'm here to talk. I don't mind being your friend, Skid. Under all that hard muscular exterior lies a sweet soul waiting to express his self."

Skid looked over at her trying to figure out if she was for real or playing, with one eyebrow raised. It was funny to him to listen to anyone speak that way about him since no one had ever done so before. He knew she was really crazy after those words and huffed heavily as he slumped back more in his seat. She rose walking around the desk to the door just to get a look out at all of the cars driving down Cicero past their business in the cut. She longed for someone, anyone to walk into the store right then, as she was bored out of her everlasting mind.

She removed the black short-sleeved jogging jacket that Amy had given her off and tossed it back behind the counter. The white tank top tucked inside of her matching thigh high jogging shorts seemed to be making her even hotter prompting her to tie it in a tight knot behind her back revealing her silky smooth skin and flat belly. Skid pretended not to watch but her ass seemed to protrude out commanding his eyes to its voluptuousness.

"Ugh, it's gotta be like ninety fucking degrees outside. How the hell did Bentley survive in this sweat shop?" She asked playfully.

"He didn't. He was too busy upstairs in the AC getting his ass busted in." Skid replied watching the sweat droplets dance off of her back and shoulders.

"Hell naw!" Red laughed as she headed back for the desk.

Skid jumped in front of her grabbing her small waist and pulling her close to him. He caught her off guard slowly moving in kissing her ever so gently on the lips. Her pussy tingled as she obliged and kissed him back loving the sweet taste of his lips even though it tasted like some kind of cognac or vodka of some sort. His kiss was so passionate and so sensual it was hard to believe that he was the hard ass that he was. It was so fanatical and so erotic and so—

SLAP!

"Motherfucka don't you ever do that again! You understand! How the fuck could you do that to me?" Red snapped.

"I…I'm sorry." Skid said wondering where that shit came from as well. He had surprised even his self with it but her body was just so tantalizing, so inviting.

"I'm with your so-called friend. Remember Messiah?"

"Yeah. Sorry. It won't happen again." He said sitting back down and staring out of the door as he wiped her sweet nectar from his lips.

Red headed back behind the desk and flopped down in the seat. She could deny the feeling that she was having inside even though she so desperately wanted to. No one had ever kissed her like that before. She looked over at him to see if she had hurt his feelings but there were no feelings displayed on his face, it was blank again. Red never wanted or felt like she asked for his warm embrace but it was nice, real nice.

Chapter 8
A & B Conversation

"Hey doc. I need to ask you some more questions and I need you to be straight up with me. I ain't got time for bullshit right now." Messiah said catching up with Alexis' attending physician.

"Yes, Mr. Torres. What is it now?" The older doctor responded feeling a tad bit fed up with Messiah and his antics.

"I just need to know if there is anything that I can do to jog her memory and speed up the process a little. You see, I need her back to 100% before I can…eh she just needs to know the truth."

"Which is?"

"None of your concern."

"Then I suggest you take your wife home and nurse her back to good health. Now she's been doing very well all this time and now that she's awake I think it would do her some good to continue treatment in her own home. That is why I am releasing her to you today." The doctor replied ripping a prescription from his note pad as he finished writing and handed it to Messiah. "The nurse is already in her room having her sign her discharge papers."

"Discharge, what ah are you even hearing yourself right now? Discharge? She isn't well enough to go home I mean she doesn't even look well enough." Messiah began freaking out.

"Calm down, Mr. Torres. I believe you will be just fine." The doctor smiled. "If it makes you feel any better, you can help to jog her memory by talking about things in her past. More than likely, she'll dream of them and hopefully it just begins to pop up."

The good doctor patted Messiah on the shoulder shooting him a sly smile then walked off past him. He wasn't about to allow Messiah to weasel his way out of taking care of his wife, like it seemed like he was trying to do. Messiah stood there watching as the doctor faded out of sight then turned in the direction of Alexis' room and headed towards it. When he got there, the sound of laughter filled the room as she was chalking it up with the older female nurse in the room who was helping her gather all of her belongings.

He couldn't see her face at all but the nurse made one sudden move out of the way revealing a soft angelic faced Alexis. She was more beautiful now with her hair in disarray, no makeup and her Cheshire cat smile than he had ever remembered. She had been fake and plastic so long that he couldn't remember the true her, the old her, the one he fell in love with. Despite her beauty he was determined to remain cold. As soon as she got her memory back she would surely treat him as badly as before if not worse and he knew that heartbreak wasn't a feeling he was prepared to face again.

"Ok, I'm here. Let's uh, get this show on the road shall we." Messiah said entering the room and grabbing the Louis Vuitton duffle bag off of the bed.

"Hey baby!" Alexis greeted him standing on her tiptoes to reach his cheek to plant a kiss. "I'm so excited to be going home. I can't wait to see what it looks like and finally get a nice hot bath."

"Yeah, uh, so we ready to go?" He turned asking the nurse.

"Yep, Alexis take seat in the wheelchair and I'll wheel you to the front door." She responded going to stand behind the chair.

As they walked out of the room and into the elevator, Alexis clung to Messiah's had not wanting to let it go. Finally on the ground floor, Messiah sought refuge from her grasp by pretending to need to readjust the bag on his shoulder. She looked around when he was done seeking to hold his hand again but he pretended not to notice walking a few steps behind them. But Alexis wasn't letting up, she reached her hand back hoping that he would grab it. Messiah looked down at it, hating the feeling of being obligated to pretend he liked her and just as he was about to give in and reach for her his cell saved the day.

"Yeah."

"Hey baby. Where are you?"

"I'm uh, I'm around. What's going on?"

"I thought you might wanted to come back up here and see ya son. I'm breast-feeding just like you wanted. So are you coming?"

"I told you I was, didn't I?" Messiah rubbed his nose and fell even further behind the group.

"Yeah. But I was just making sure, baby. I miss, I mean, we miss you."

"Aye B. Don't get this shit twisted aight. We just parents, keepin' it cool. I thought we discussed this." Messiah spoke quietly into the phone.

"We did. I understand. I'm just being nice is all." Braze said looking down into her son's high yellow face. "I just wanted to take some pictures and stuff."

"Well when I get back there we can do all that. Cool?"

"Cool." The sound of disappointment resonated throughout her response.

She hung up the hospital phone lightly even though she didn't want to do so. Her first mind was to launch the motherfucka across the room and scream at the top of her lungs. All she could think about was getting the hell out of that bed so she could go run up behind Messiah. She figured that when the baby was born he would treat her like the queen that she was. She wanted him to quit fucking with every bitch on the side and wife her for good. Braze felt like she had put in enough time and work that she should've been getting the utmost respect, but all she seemed to be getting was the cold shoulder. *If it's that bitch, Red, she will fucking pay.* Braze thought sucking her teeth.

"Agh!" Braze clenched her stapled belly as she rose from the bed slowly to return the MJ back to his bunker.

He was sleeping soundly for a newborn, which she loved since her stitches were giving her fever right then.

"Nurse! Nurse!" Braze yelled through the intercom as she pushed the button on the remote next to the bed.

"Yes."

"My stitches hurt so bad."

"Okay, I'm coming."

Braze eased back into the bed trying to get in before the nurse saw her. She remembered that the doctor told her she shouldn't be walking on her first day and to try to wait until tomorrow, but she was naturally stubborn. It was all she could do to get better faster and get in the streets. Her crippled state only held her back from the man she loved and the status she so desperately needed to claim. There was no way she was going to be the scrub her sister was. She would be better, greater, not the low level gold-digging whore her sister was, or their mother even.

"Okay now honey you know you ain't supposed to be movin' about." The nurse said busting in catching Braze in the act of scooting back into the bed. "Didn't you hear what the doctor said?"

"Yes, I heard what he said but I had to put my baby back in the bed. What you want me to buzz the intercom every time I need y'all?"

"Uh yeah that's the idea." The nurse laughed. "Honey, that's what we get paid for. Besides you just had a C-section, you should be resting all you can. We take the baby and by the second day you should be able to move about more freely."

"Why does it take so long?" Braze whined.

"Child, because it does. Hell your body has just gone through a great ordeal. Even though many people don't realize it, having a baby is a major thing. People die from having babies."

"Die from having babies? Well I ain't dead yet and I'm trying to get the hell outta here."

"Why? So you can run up behind your baby's daddy? Does he have another girl?" The nurse asked pumping a shot of Demerol into her IV.

"Yeah, I mean no. I mean…ugh. I just wanna get out of here okay!"

"Well honey, right now you need to just lie back and enjoy the relaxation because in a few days you'll be home with a screaming baby. Nighty night." The nurse smiled tucking her blanket in a bit.

Her words were echoed and slurred to Braze as her head began to bobble from the effects of the pain medication. She wasn't trying to go to sleep wanting to hold her head up high but it was becoming virtually impossible. The nurse walked over to the baby staring down into the bunker thinking how beautiful he was to have a dumb ass, young, and naïve skank for a mother. Even though she didn't know Braze from anywhere, she took her first impressions seriously and that's all that she could gather from their conversation.

She was about to wheel the baby out of the room when she looked up at the clock on the wall. "Oops, almost 1 o'clock. Almost didn't get you any dinner sent down for you. Not that you'd eat it from the looks of this lunch but if your ass get hungry enough you'll eat it."

The nurse ran her fingers through her bob cut deciding to leave the baby in the room while went back to the nurse's station to put Braze's dinner order in really quickly. Instead of closing the room door she decided to leave it open just in case the baby started crying. Braze was the only patient in her room and no one would hear the baby otherwise. The door hadn't even closed all the way when a large hand pushed it open. Braze was still in bobble head mode when the tall figure came walking in the room and up to her bed. Her vision was blurred and the room felt steamy hot.

"Hey there, Braze. How you feeling?"

"Wha…who…"

"Naw, don't speak. I just came to congratulate you on your new arrival." The figure walked over to MJ looking over into his bunker as he stirred in his swaddled blanket. "He's a beaut, isn't he?"

"Don't touch…my fucking ba—by" Braze's words were drawn out and slurred.

She tried to rise up from the bed nearly ripping her IV out of her arm. The pinch settled her back down and so did the medication. She leaned back against the pillow struggling to find the nurse's remote with her hand but she ended up pushing it down on the side of the bed. She tried to widen her eyes to see if she could get a clear visual of who was hovering their breath all over her son. She thought it best to squint her eyes and found herself still squirming in the bed to move. Whoever it was made her feel very uneasy.

"You know you should really take it easy. You don't want to rip your sutures." The voice rang out in laughter. "Looks like your gauzes need changing."

"The fuck are…you?"

"Who I am? Oh you don't remember me. Should I feel bad because you don't remember your old friend?" The voice came as close to her face as the hair on her head. "Can you see me now?"

"P…P…"

"Yeah. Hey baby. Do me a favor. Tell ya girl, Red, we ain't over and I'm coming for what's mine, ya heard?" The figure laughed low pitched and sinisterly as he galloped slowly towards the door. "See ya around kid. Oh, I'll get that nurse for ya too."

"Excuse me." The nurse said bumping into the man as he exited the room.

"No, excuse me. Uh, Ms. Braze might need her gauzes changed. Thought I'd let you know." He smiled widely.

"Oh ok." The nurse hesitated awkwardly with a raised eyebrow. "Thanks, I'll tend to them."

As the nurse walked in the room, she noticed Braze struggling to get some words out of her mouth. She chalked it up as the medicine making her woozy and paid it no mind as she took a look at her sutures. Braze leaned back against her pillow again and let out a deep breath before closing her eyes and allowing her head to fall to the left.

"P...P..."

Chapter 9
The Married Life

Messiah helped Alexis into the truck as she leaned on his shoulders for a little support. She looked into his face to see if she could find a sense of happiness or comfort but she found only emptiness. He quickly closed her door then entered the car and pulled off. The car was silent the whole twenty minute drive to their Willowbrook suburban home. Alexis wanted to speak but she unable to let the words fly out of her mouth. The only thing she could do was look over at him from time to time to see check his facial expression. Once they pulled into the driveway of their big beautiful million-dollar home. She gasped unable to believe they were doing it that big.

"That…that's our home?" Alexis asked with her mouth agape.

"Yep. Let's go. I'll get your bags." Messiah replied nonchalantly.

"I can't believe I live here. Baby, what do we do for a living?" She turned and asked closing the car door behind her.

"Uh, well I run a successful storage facility in Oak Lawn not far from the hospital we just left and you, well you do nothing."

"I don't do anything? Oh well we have got to change that. There is no way I'm about to be the wife of such a successful handsome man and not put in on this and help you out." She smiled happily walking up to the front door with him. "Wait, am I a stay at home mom?"

"No, Alexis. We don't have kids."

"Oh…" She wanted to ask more questions but it seemed as if Messiah wasn't interested in answering them.

"Well the grand tour in a nutshell, we have five bedrooms and seven bathrooms. No we really didn't need all that but you had to have it so I got it for you. Uh, You notice which one is the master bedroom because it's the biggest room in the house with floor to ceiling bay windows. Mahogany wood floors throughout the house and you make me pay a maid to clean so you don't have to worry about that either." Messiah said like he was running down a list.

"Do I cook?"

"Ha! I wish." He backed down once he saw the discerning look on her face. "Sorry."

"No, I mean its okay. I get it. I was a spoiled rich wife who was lazy." Alexis sat down on the huge red Camden sectional sitting in the middle of the living room.

She began to sob heavily covering her eyes in embarrassment. It was crazy that she was so blessed but the person she didn't remember she was wasn't appreciative of any of it. It her hurt her deeply that she could be such a selfish person when there were people out there who didn't have half of the things she did.

"Just tell me the truth," Alexis looked up with her face drenched in tears. "did we have marital problems? Are we divorcing?"

Messiah looked at her wide-eyed. He knew this was his chance to finally get out of this marriage once and for all. It was wrong and he felt bad but he knew that this was the only way. It needed to happen while she was her sweet self because once the demon came back she would never divorce him. Secretly he thanked God for this opportunity.

"Uh, yeah. You actually cheated on me with my big brother, Danger. We haven't been happy for years." Messiah tried to sound as distraught as could be without an ounce of the excitement he was actually feeling.

"I can't believe this. So what now? Do I leave? Where do I go? I'm broke I have no money, hell I don't even know how to so shit. Oh my God!!" Alexis began to freak out.

"Hey, hey. Just calm down alright. I wouldn't leave you out there like that now. I've got a nice alimony package set up for you even though you cheated and it's for the first twelve months after the divorce is finalized. So don't worry okay." He walked over kneeling to wipe tears from her eyes. "Everything's going to be ok. In the mean time why don't you sleep in one of the guests bedrooms."

"When do we meet with the lawyers?"

"Next week. Why?"

"Because I don't want to make your life anymore miserable than I already have." Alexis walked off from him taking her duffle bag and headed upstairs.

Messiah sighed heavily rubbing his head feeling bad about what he had just done. He didn't want to hurt her feelings and for that matter had never seen Alexis so sincere. The tears that flowed from her eyes were actually as genuine as the black Gucci patent leather shoes he was wearing. He picked his face up off the floor and headed up the wide staircase to the first guest room where he could hear her moving around in.

Knock. Knock.

"Hey. Can I come in?"

"No please. Just leave me be right now. Okay?"

"Alexis, we need to talk."

"I think we've talked enough."

Messiah exhaled deeply. "I'm comin' in girl."

"Messiah go away! I can't seem to do anything right. Out of everything that I don't remember, the only thing that I do remember is you but apparently I'm losing that too. What the fuck is wrong with me?"

"Look, maybe you are looking at this the wrong way. You seem like a better person now than I've ever known. So maybe you should take this as a first step to starting your brand new life as a better individual." Messiah snapped hoping to get through her chaotic mood swing.

"I remember you though. That has to mean something."

"You remember the good times though. That was the beginning of us. The end of us is coming to an end." Messiah sat next to her on the bed as she plopped down covering her face.

"I can't look at you."

"Why?"

"Cause you're my husband and I can't even touch you or hold you or have you hold me or nothing. Do you know how that feels?" Alexis sat up looking deep into his eyes.

"Yeah, actually I do. I went through it for years. I wanted to hold you and tell you how much I loved you. I wanted to make bad ass babies with you." He said as they laughed. "But we grew apart."

"No I cheated and with your fucking brother! Oh my God!"

"Lex, I'm over it and you should too. I want nothing but happiness for you. So just make sure you do that, move forward and be happy. Okay?" He said pinching her chin playfully.

"So…there's no way we could work this out? Huh?" Alexis asked looking pitifully up into his eyes.

"I really seriously doubt it."

"Why have you moved on?"

Messiah hesitated a bit. He didn't want to add more fuel to the fire but he knew it would be the icing on the cake to solidify their divorce for good. "Yeah, sort of."

"Wow." Alexis ran her fingers through her elongated weave. "Well, what's her name?"

"Redina. Well we call her Red."

"We. So I know her? Are we friends?"

"No, no nothing like that. I meant we as in my friends."

"Oh. Well ok, I guess. I guess I can't interfere with your happiness then. Are you…happy?" She asked placing her hand on his shoulder for effect and poking her tits out in front of her.

"I'd like to think so. Yes."

Alexis retreated her chest in disappointment. She wondered exactly how long his love for her had been gone but felt it was pointless to ask now. Tears continued to flow from her eyes but she wasn't balling or hysterical, she was silent. Messiah saw that as the calm before the storm. For some reason it frightened him thinking that the news would trigger the bitchy evil her to sprout back up like the leaves on a tree at the first sight of Spring.

"Well, I think you should leave me be for while. I just need some time to think." Alexis said lying down on the oversized fluffy bed cuddling up to one of the plush purple pillows.

"Okay. I've got some business to handle but I'll be back in a few hours." Messiah said looking at her watching as tears continued to water her chunky cheeks.

"Yep."

"Are you sure you gonna be alright? I mean, could I get you anything?" Messiah backpedaled.

"No, really. I'll be fine. Just go." Alexis focused her eyes on the outside landscape so she wouldn't see him leave.

"Alright well there's food downstairs in the fridge and you know, just, make yourself at home."

"You tryin' to be funny?"

"What, naw naw. I didn't mean anything by it. I just mean...just if you get hungry...never mind." Messiah headed towards the door then turned to look back at a sad Alexis balled up on the bed hugging a pillow like it was her best friend. "Okay well, I'm gone."

"You said that."

"Okay…okay." Messiah finally stripped his eyes away from watching her and walked out the room.

Alexis didn't flinch, listening closely for the sound of the door closing. Once she got her confirmation that he was gone she broke down, crying and screaming as loud as she wanted. Not only was her heart broken but also she felt rejected and abandoned. She was in the most fragile state of her life but found herself alone. As her tears fell she wondered how horrible would it be if she tried to fix her marriage all in a week's time. *Could I do it?* She thought as she sat up lost in deep thought.

She raced out of the room and down the hall to the master bedroom. In the back of her mind she knew exactly where the room was without having to look for it. At the moment she didn't realize it but it was a suppressed memory resurfacing. Her eyes widened at the gloriousness of the room from the gigantic bed in the far corner of the room to the "his and hers" closets that sat on the opposite side. The top of the closets adorned specific his and hers insignia written in the most beautiful script she had ever seen and sparkling like diamonds.

"I can't believe all of this is mine." She said as she entered her walk in closet marveling at all of the luxurious clothes, coats, and shoes.

She stripped down to her bare skin and walked past all of the hanging clothes with her hands out gently rubbing them as she past. The back of the closet held racks and racks of shoes. There were so many shoes she couldn't even decide as to which ones to try on first until a bright shiny red pair caught her eye. She slipped them on with ease the turned for a model walk as her tits bounced and her ass swayed in rhythm. As she rubbed her hands back across the clothes she stopped in front of a blue jean crop jacket that was too cute to her. She put it on then went to stand in the mirror.

"Yep. Fix my hair, throw on some makeup, cook some dinner and remind you who loves you baby. I do."

Chapter 10
Red Drama

"Awe shit my bad, Red. I swear I didn't mean it man you just…you just looked so damn good right there." Skid said wiping the sweat from his forehead along with the drool from his mouth.

"Oh my God. If that shit gets back to Messiah, we'll never be together. Don't you have any restraint?" Red snapped still wiping her lips hoping to get the scent of him off of her.

"Look, I said I was sorry alright. I ain't gonna beg or plead with you or nothing. You either take it or leave it."

"Sheesh. Next time give a girl a heads up, would ya?"

"There won't be a next time."

"Thank you. Thank you for that, Skid." She grabbed a grape Crush soda out of the mini fridge and popped it open.

"Well you ain't gotta worry about me letting this get to Meech, ight? He don't need to know this shit."

Red couldn't bring herself to respond. She sipped on her soda and focused in on the music playing on the computer screen, rocking back and forth in the swivel chair. No matter how hard she tried, she couldn't get the sweet taste of his lips off of hers. Her heart knew she didn't like the kiss but her pussy, which was now moist from gooeyness and not sweat, spoke a different story. She exhaled lowering her head into her hands on the desk then lifted up startled from an excessive banging on the office window.

"Aye motherfuckas! Where is he, huh? Where's my motherfucking man?" Maxwell shouted storming into the office.

"Man who the fuck are you?" Skid snapped reaching behind his back for his nine.

"Nigga you know who I am! Where the fuck is my man?"

"Okay, nobody knows who you're talking about. I think you've got the wrong place, buddy." Red said with her hands extended trying to diffuse the problem.

Maxwell had a short cut with purple on one side and yellow on the other. His tight booty shorts made his plumped ass stick out like a sore thumb making Red jealous that his was bigger than hers. He had his tank top tied in the back and was wearing a fresh pair of Air Force Ones. Even though he didn't have long hair he kept flicking the air around his ear like he did, imaginarily flicking it out of his way. Maxwell put up his dukes; ready to get it in with Skid if he didn't answer his question.

"Oh!" Skid laughed. "Now I remember you."

"Yeah motherfucka now you getting the picture huh?

"What's going on here?" Red asked confusingly.

"Ya boy here is Bentley's fun boy or should I say fuck boy." Skid laughed.

"Oh yeah. Now I know who you are. Yeah you was the dude I caught in the room with him over here, right?"

"That shit don't matter." Maxwell snapped. "Where the fuck is my baby? He ain't answerin' his phone and he usually calls me to come over in the morning but he ain't did none of that."

"Oh, well I don't know where the fuck that nigga at." Skid said taking his seat back in the chair.

Red covered her mouth. Of course they knew exactly what happened to Bentley but there was no way in hell they were about to tell him. She sat back down in the chair keeping her head down figuring she needed to let Skid do all the talking. Maxwell began hyperventilating as he wiped a mass of sweat bullets from his face. Red could tell by the eerie deranged look in his face that he was about to do something that would either land him in the hospital or in the same position as Bentley. She knew he was in over his head.

"I think it's time for you to go dude." Red blurted standing back up and leaning across the counter to touch Maxwell's shoulder.

"Get your hands off me." Maxwell snapped as he snatched away. "I ain't going no motherfucking where until I somebody tell me where my boo is at."

"Man don't nobody know where that nigga at so you need to bounce, homie!" Skid became agitated.

"Naw motherfucka you bounce!" Maxwell lunged at Skid, scratching and clawing into his face like a nigga cat.

He demanded answers or justice for his lover. Red jumped over the counter screaming at the men pleaded for them to stop acting like Neanderthals but it was no use. They were locked tight in the middle of their tussle and weren't letting go. She knew it was best not to get caught in the middle of a huge grizzly bear and a damn gazelle. All she could do was plead from the background as she leaned on the door shaking her head the sight.

"What the hell is going on in here?" Messiah roared angrily snatching the door handle from under Red's arm almost making her fall as he entered.

The two men were so engaged in their brawl that neither heard him yell nor noticed the bells above the door ding as he came in. Messiah yanked Maxwell up by his mini afro releasing Skid from the headlock he had him in. He shook his head at Skid wondering how in the hell did a mouse defeat a lion. Red tried her best not to laugh but the distraught look on Maxwell's face as he clenched up was priceless.

"Why are you in my place of business bringing noise?" Messiah snarled aggressively into Maxwell's ear.

"I was...I was just looking for my boo, Bentley. Sir." Maxwell almost shitted on his self and was mildly aroused at the same time.

"That nigga was fired last night. So look somewhere else. If I catch you around here again, I'm gon' put my nine in your eye and pretend to have turrets. Ya heard." Messiah replied before releasing him.

Maxwell was a ghost in the wind. They didn't even see his feet leave the floor as he ran up out of the office. Skid sat down in the chair knowing and awaiting the bomb that was coming. He just kept his head down hoping that the nigga got the shit over with quickly.

"Red, baby, when you close this place tonight make sure everything is locked up and then head to the crib. I'll meet you there later on. I gotta handle some business but I will be to see you alright?"

"What the fuck, Messiah? You rippin' and runnin' the streets for these tricks now? Look you keep begging me to stay, remember? I was going to leave you and you begged me to stay."

"I know."

"So if you know then why the fuck do I feel like you playin' me to the left for these hoes you don't even care about? Got me sitting up in this hot ass office all day and shit. You got me fucked up, Messiah."

"Man, I ain't playin' you for anybody. I'm just askin' for your cooperation. You know what's going on, it ain't like I'm lying to you. If I didn't care about you I wouldn't be here. Sometimes the everybody gotta take one for the team, right?"

"Why its gotta be me though?"

"Red, quit tripin'. I just need to organize this mess and once its done then its done. Just be patient for me. Aight?" Messiah said grabbing her chin softly.

He turned back focusing his energy and thoughts back on Skid and trying to get out of Red's whining. He knew she was feeling salty because of all the things that were going on and her being neglected. But he didn't feel like dealing with her right then. He crossed his arms waiting for to be a man about his and look him in the eye but his stiff demeanor made it perfectly clear that he had planned to keep his head down until her left.

"Dude. You really gonna sit there and act like I ain't here, man?" Messiah said repositioning and planting his feet firmly on the black and white checkerboard floor.

"Man, Meech. We need to talk man."

"You motherfucking right we need to talk." Messiah's language sent off the vibe that he was beyond pissed.

"Naw, man. I mean we need to talk."

"Okay. Talk. Talk about how you got all this noise up in my business. Talk about you almost having your ass handed to you by a frail ass fun boy. Huh? Talk about that." Messiah thumped his nose with his thumb.

"Dude, I ain't got no control over what the next motherfucka come up in here on. I told his ass to step, he ain't listen." Skid licked his lips and stood towering over Messiah. "And I ain't get my ass handed to me. I was chill."

"Yeah, I bet you were. Meanwhile customers comin' in and out the business seein' this shit." Messiah snapped. "Respect my shit!"

"Man, look you got worser problems than that surrounding you."

"Skid, I don't even wanna hear that shit man.

"Meech, I'm dead ass man."

"And I said I don't wanna hear that shit right now man. Now, leave ya piece with Red and take your ass on back on to the tip, boy. You need to sleep that battery acid off."

Messiah turned back towards Red staring her in her eyes. It was his way of letting Skid know that the conversation was dead. Skid smacked his lips taking his nine from the back of his pants and damn near slamming it on the counter then walked out the door. He screeched his tires, as he pulled off pissed at how he had just got treated. Messiah brushed it off siting that he had too much bullshit on his plate already.

"Aye, hold me down alright. You know how to use this?" He asked sliding the piece over in front of her.

"What do you think?" She asked picking it up loving the weight of it in her hands.

"Aight, then. I'll be back to pick you up at closing. We'll do…something."

He waved as he walked out of the door and hopped back in his black Escalade. Apart of her wanted to pick the nine up and aim it for his head but the other part of her halted that idea. Messiah knew what he was doing when he talked to her in his sexy sly tone. He thought he had her in the bag manipulating her to do whatever he wanted. It was true he loved her but he was torn and it showed all over his face.

Red flopped back down in the computer chair fanning herself seeking relief from the heat. Dru Hill wailed about not making love anymore and the words only made her feel worse. She felt like she shouldn't have been sitting in a hot ass office with no air conditioning, she should've been riding the streets with him setting things straight and getting his money back on top. It didn't seem like he was as all about his business as he had claimed to be.

She ransacked the file cabinet drawers looking for any files of the business but found no one. It hit her that they all had to be downstairs in his office. Her thoughts focused immediately on figuring out how she could get those files. They were her only connection to getting her man's business back to the thriving state that it was in before Zadie and her minions sunk their claws into it.

"This man just don't know what he has, but I'm gon' show him." She spoke as she bobbed her head to the music.

Her plan was about to be set in motion and now all she needed was a way in. She leaned her head back on the seat and as she looked up to smile she heard a knocking on the window behind her. The blinds were closed so she wasn't able to see who was out there but a huge shadowy figure graced its darkness upon it. Her hand unconsciously grabbed the nine from off the desk and secured it to her side. The figure didn't move it just stood there. It was as if it was waiting for her to make her move. It could have been anybody, even Messiah but she wasn't about to take the chance.

Securing her piece making sure it was cocked and loaded, she walked around to the front of the desk to put some space between her and the figure. As she watched it, she tried not to blink so that she could see which way it went if it decided to dip off. The figure appeared to be swaying in such a way as if it was toying with her or dancing to the music that she was listening to.

"Enough of this shit." She said as she headed out the door with the piece to her side.

She leaned her back against the wall scaling it like she was an experienced detective. At the corner of the building, she closed her eyes and took a deep breath knowing that whoever was around the corner had better have a good reason for being by that window or it was lights out for their ass.

"Don't move bitch!" Red yelled pointing the nine at a tall bush being blown by the wind.

Chapter 11
Braze & Messiah

"Hey little man. It's me your daddy. You're so handsome just like your daddy. I can't wait to teach you how to ride a bike and play football. You gotta play football. It's the manliest sport around. But you can play whatever you want to play as long as you remember to never give up. Daddy's gonna make sure you have everything you need and most of what you want. If it takes every breath in my body..."

Messiah lowered MJ back into the hospital grade bassinet then leaned over to kiss his forehead. His angelic face was so light and he was as still as a mannequin, sleeping heavily from his long hard day. He made sure that he didn't mess up his swaddled blanket tightening it up in the places just below his chin where it had unraveled. It was hard for him to leave the room with but he knew his little boy needed some rest. He looked around at the other eight babies in the room all sleeping soundly in their beds, thinking that they were all tiny blessings in the making. It was then that he realized he wanted out of the drug business. He wanted to make his business completely legit so that his son could something worth bragging about and not feel ashamed. He didn't want his son to turn out like him.

As he left the room and headed down the hall to Braze's room he noticed that he had a few missed calls on his cell. They were from Red. He shook his head returning it back into the hideout that was his pocket not wanting to talk to her while he was there. Braze was knocked out cold it seemed as he walked in her room and up to the bed gazing down on her. She had her mouth open with drool creeping down the left side of her cheek. It was kind of cute.

"Braze. B! Wake up."

"Huh, uh, oh. What?"

"I'm back."

"Damn. It sure took you long enough." Braze retorted as she wiped the smidgen of drool still dripping down her chin.

"Yeah, told you I had business that I needed to handle. I just came from seeing the little man."

"Oh yeah. What was he doing?"

"Sleepin', you know, just chillin'. Messiah replied as he removed the body cross strap from his torso and placed the stuffed baby bag in the narrow pearl colored closet behind him. "I got you some clothes for you and the baby up in here."

"You brought us new clothes?"

"Well I just wanted to be the one to buy him a new fit to come home in and then I realized you didn't have anything either. It's just some little stuff, ya know." He chuckled modestly.

"Oh my God! My baby was thinking about us. I know we are going to love it baby, thank you." Braze's face lit up like a Ferris Wheel at night.

"Yeah. But I had to get the lil' man something." Messiah thumbed his nose as he sniffed.

"Oh, thanks babe! I wanna see him so bad but my fucking stitches hurt. They took him outta here because that nurse doped me up so good I wouldn't have heard the building blow up if it did."

"Oh yeah. Don't be getting addicted to that mess." Messiah said taking a seat in the leather chair over on the side of the bed as he peeked out of the window.

"Nigga, now how could I get addicted to that shit? It's just medicine, baby. It ain't like its heroine or something."

"People get addicted off prescriptions everyday. Don't act like you don't know th—"

"Are you serious? Why the hell would I do that? I mean, I've got so much to look forward to right?"

"B., don't start that shit again and don't patronize me like I'm stupid or something." The inflection in Messiah's voice was becoming more intense.

"Don't snap on me. I'm not fucking with you. I'm just saying I'm clean alright."

"Naw you lucky MJ is clean. That's what's lucky." Messiah snapped sarcastically.

"I don't even want to talk about that shit anymore, baby. I want to talk about us."

"Braze, there is no us. How many time do we have to go through this, fifteen or fifteen million?"

"Wha… But I thought that since we have MJ now that—"

"That what? That I would come running to you and want to start a family with you? It's never going to happen, Braze. We have a baby, a son together. But that's it!"

"I heard you, damn. You ain't gotta holla." Braze snarled turning her lip as far up as it would go. "I just thought that us being together would be as easy as breathing."

"If you heard me then you sure as hell weren't listening." Messiah stood hovering over her bed.

"You know, why is it so hard for you to believe that you that we could be good together? We could really fucking have something, Meech. Why are you fightin' it?" Braze asked with puppy dog eyes.

"You don't even know me, B. You think you do but you don't."

"I know that you love to make your soup really hot then put ice cubes in it to cool it down. I know that you can't start your day without a cup of coffee from your Keurig machine. I know that whenever you need encouragement or a shoulder to cry on you hop in my bed for comfort." Braze snapped gritting her teeth with tears flowing down her face. "And I know that we loved each other enough to give each other a perfect beautiful little baby boy. Are you not willing to give him the family he deserves?"

Messiah lowered his head at her last remark feeling like it hit home. She knew MJ meant more to him than life itself and he was willing to do anything to make him happy. He turned hawking at her as if he wanted to slap the taste out of her mouth for trying to manipulate home. Playing mind games were not something that Messiah handled to well.

"He definitely deserves a family, B. But I'm just not sure if it should be this one."

"You killed my fucking sister, Meech. Don't you think you owe me that much?" Brazen lowered her head into her bosom speaking in a very dark and raspy, sinister voice.

"What? First of all, no I didn't and second of all you couldn't even stand her ass!"

"So what! She was still the only real family I had left."

"Look, Braze, I didn't come here to argue with you about shit. I came to see my son and to make sure you were straight. That's it. If you can't deal with us not being together in front of Mj I'll have him picked up everyday so I can see him. You ain't gotta even see me."

"Messiah that's not what I want. I...just forget it."

"That's the best thing you said since I've been sitting here." Messiah rubbed the stress out of his chin. "I'm out. Its getting late and I ain't even ate none today. I'll holla at you tomorrow."

"Yep." Braze crossed her arms as she looked away.

"Kiss my son for me when they bring him back." He said hitting the door.

"Kiss him yourself when you bring your ass back here." Brazen mumbled.

She was beyond furious. In her mind, that talk with Messiah went better than the one that had just happened. Her lips pouted like a three year old and her eyebrows curled over as she struggled to calm down from his words. His total disregard for the state of their relationship plagued her being. It annoyed her that her body was restricted to the hospital bed she was in. Messiah's absence from her and her son wouldn't make his heart grow fonder, that much was clear. Braze picked up the nurse's buzzer pressing harder than ever.

"Yes?"

"Hi. Um, can you bring me my baby please? I would like to feed him." She said biting her lip.

"Oh, sure! I'll be in there in a minute." The nurse answered back through the intercom.

Braze rolled her eyes trying to be patient but she knew that nurse did what she wanted to do when she wanted to do it. So it completely surprised her when the nurse came walking through her room door pushing MJ happily. She had stored quite a few bottles of unopened Enfamil under the baby bunker including diapers and wipes as well.

"Ok, Ms. Braze. I have set you up for the whole night so you are good to go."

"What? What do you mean? I can leave now?" Braze exhaled anxiously.

"Uh no. I thought we talked about this earlier. No, hun you're going to be here for at least another day or two just so that we can make sure that your stitches don't get infected. Girl you can die from that." The nurse said checking Braze's IV.

"Two days? Ugh! I hate hospitals. They make you feel so helpless."

"Girl, I'd rather be here sometimes. When you restin', its like you're on a vacation." The nurse side eyed her as she headed for the door. "So if you need anything or any help throughout the night for the baby, you know what to do."

Braze could care less about the fake smile the nurse shot at her before she left. She was more concerned with dealing with MJ for a whole night straight. Her inexperience with babies scared her even though she got the breast-feeding down packed. It would have been nice to have Messiah there to help her out and do things a father would do on the baby's first night home. A single tear formed then slowly crept down her golden cheek realizing that not only was her pride hurt but also her soul as well. She reached over grabbing her cell phone out of the drawer of the nightstand.

"Hello. What you doing?"

"Shit. Drinking. The fuck you calling me for?"

"Oh. Um, Meech told me to call you when I was ready. He told me he called you and told you all about it." Braze bit her lip, watching the room door. "He didn't call you?"

"If he did I wouldn't be asking you that question."

"Hehe. Right. Well, um you supposed to come pick me up and take me to his house."

"Huh? His house? Man, I know that nigga ain't tell me know shit like that. I need to call this fool."

"No! I mean, he told me that he would be busy and not answering his phone so he just wanted me to come."

"Yeah. And the hospital releasing you that early? You just had the baby."

"Yeah well, what can I say? I'm a fast healer. Anyway me and the baby are ready so are you on your way or what?" Braze paused allowing the awkward silence to fill the dead air. "I mean, I could just all Meech and tell him you can't do it."

"Naw, naw. I'll be there in ten."

"Okay. I'll be waiting outside the main entrance."

Once Braze hung up she maneuvered slowly out of bed being sure not to disrupt her stitches and scurried over to the closet. She leaned in briefly gazing down upon MJ's angelic face. *His whole life is sleeping.* She thought as she whisked open the zipper on the brown and green Disney's Mickey Mouse checkered baby bag. She pulled out a pair of pink Victoria Secret

Pink jogging pants with matching tank and jacket. Her lips curled up feeling like a man who isn't in love with a female is not going to buy her Victoria Secret anything. She knew he had some kind of love for her and just needed it busted open for him to admit it.

She slid off the hospital gown and slid the cotton panties the nurse's provided to her earlier with a thick huge pad to soak up her bleeding. Then she dressed in her new outfit post haste. She didn't want to wake MJ by putting on his clothes so she removed the clothes from the bag and put them in her jacket to resemble the pregnant belly she once adorned. Gently, Braze extracted the baby from the baby bunker and placed him inside of the bag only zipping it half way to allow air to seep in and out. The remaining milk, diapers and wipes she stuffed deep down in her makeshift belly to give it a little extra plumpness.

After she slipped the bag over her head and across her body smoothly, she snatched one of the receiving blankets and wrapped it around her head Ericka Badu style forming the round knot in the back so the hospital issue printed lines would not be visible. When she had collected everything, she took a deep breath, closed her eyes, and headed for the door. The nurse's station was no less than a few feet away from her room door so she knew that at least of them would see her but she had hoped they wouldn't recognize her. There was no time to peek around outside of the door, cause that was sure way of looking suspicious. Instead she clenched her cell in her hand and bolted out, speed walking like she was in a marathon heading straight for the elevators without looking back.

"Com' on. Com' on!" Braze snarled silently as she repeatedly beat the down button of the elevator.

She could hear the cackling of the nurses at the station and was certain none of them had seen her. She was careful to close the room door behind her and figured as long as no buzzing came from that room she would not be found out for hours. By then she would be long gone. On the bottom floor she raced towards the exit and prayed that Skid was out there so she wouldn't have to wait long. Her phone began vibrating as she pushed through the revolving doors.

"Yeah."

"Yeah. I tried to call Meech and he ain't answering and shit so I'm outside. I hope your ass for real on this shit, B. 'Cause if you ain't you know that's your ass, right." Skid asked.

Braze hung up the phone as she carefully removed MJ from the bag before she made it to Skid's truck. She held him in her arms as if she had done so the entire time. She single-handedly removed the clothes and baby items from under her jacket and tossed them into the bag with ease. Knock. Knock. Her fingers tapped on the passenger side window softly as he popped the lock allowing her to climb in.

"Where the fuck you come from? I ain't even see you come out." He asked looking down at MJ. "I thought they was supposed to wheel you out or some shit."

"Yeah, yeah, yeah. Whatever man. Just drive."

Chapter 12
Motherhood?

"Hi, sir. Are you the father?"

"Uh, yes sir. I'm the father. Is everything okay?"

"Well, there was a lot of bleeding. Your wife is going to be just fine, though we've got her heavily sedated." The doctor answered.

"And the baby?"

"Well, the baby is a bouncing young man." He smiled holding out his hand.

"Man? I have a son? I HAVE A SON!" Danger yelled in excitement. "Yes!"

The medical staff looked at him, clapping and smiling for him as he raised his hand to thank them like he was the king of the castle. He extended his hand to oblige the doctor's, shaking firmly. "Thanks doc. Can I see them?"

"Well the baby is still being tended to but they'll bring him in her room in a few minutes. Like I said your wife is heavily sedated but you may see her." The doctor held on to his hand not allowing him to walk off. "There are a couple of things though."

"Well lay it on me doc. I need to know."

"Since your wife was only seven months when she gave birth that does consider your baby to be a preemie. Which means he will have to remain in the hospital a little while longer than normal. Now it would be just until we can make sure his organs and everything are okay."

"Most definitely. I mean, whatever we gotta do."

The men shook again as Danger broke the link sprinted to Amy's room. He entered looking down on her bobble head knowing that the medicine was definitely kicking in. She was just as beautiful as the day he met her so many years ago. Making her his wife would not only be the best thing for their family but also the right thing. He kneeled down beside her bed and took her hand in his giving it a gentle peck then wiping away any access wetness.

"Babe, from the moment I saw you, I knew you were the one. I loved you and I didn't even know you and I love you still. I was a fool and a dummy. Could you ever forgive?" His words rolled of his tongue as if it were wet paint to a dry wall. "I guess what I'm trying to ask here is…will you marry me?"

The dark skinned nurse began blushing feeling as though his message could have been for her. It was said so beautifully and sincerely that she nearly said yes her damn self. She finished checking the monitors currently hooked up to Amy's arms then slid her big boned body from around the side of her bed and walked over tapping Danger on the shoulder.

"After that kind of proposal, if she won't I will." She winked as she left the room smiling brightly.

Amy nodded around, grunting and moaning almost incoherently. She pulled together a few words but nothing that Danger picked up on right away. He was only paying attention and looking for one word to be said. Nothing else mattered to him except hearing the very thing he knew he needed to feel better about himself in this situation. It seemed as though if he had never had that argument with Amy she might never had gone into preterm labor and had the baby way too early. It was his fault and he had to make things right with her no matter what.

"So, what'll you say babe? Will you marry a nigga or what?" Danger honestly waited for an answer.

Deep inside Amy heard every word that he was asking. She was in and out of it with the medicine doping her up and making her feel woozy but for the most part her hearing worked just fine. She had no intentions on answering him in her current state or giving him words that he might have misinterpreted. The truth was that after all of this she had no plans or desires to marry him anymore. Especially not after learning of his views on a woman's role in his life and certainly not since the baby was dead. It was a sad thing to admit to herself but there was no denying that she was happy that the baby was dead and they could go their separate ways and move on with their lives. In her mind, she and he were through.

"Hey mommy and daddy or newlyweds, whatever you wanna be right now. I brought your little boy." The nurse said dancing as she walked in the room. "Now this is a one time thing any other time you guys gotta go to the NICU to see him. But we wanted to give mom a look before she passed out."

"Hey babe. Look. Look it's our son. Its our boy." Danger smiled.

"Our...b?"

"Yeah babe! He's okay. You did it babe! He's okay." Danger tried to get her to sit up but she wouldn't budge.

Amy wished the medicine would kick in faster so she could imagine she dreamt everything he had just said. Her eyes wanted to bulge but they were too weak and heavy. She shook her head and waved her arms flagrantly pushing him away. He took the hint feeling like she need her rest and walked over to the incubator.

"Awe you should see him, babe. He's just how I imagined a baby to be. He's soft and gentle and tiny and... Can I hold him?" He asked looking up at the nurse.

"Well he's got to stay in there and we want to give it a week or two to get his body fat and everything up so just be patient. You'll be able to snuggle him and everything soon." The nurse assured Danger. "Now say bye bye."

"Bye bye lil' dude. Daddy will see you soon." Danger said waving as she wheeled the incubator back out of the door.

"Babe you should have seen him. He's beautiful. I thought we were having a girl but we had a boy. Isn't that great?"

"Mmmmm." Amy mumbled angry.

"I'll be right back babe. I'm just gonna call Meech real quick." Danger said as he scurried out the door and down the hall. "Yo Meech. What up fool?"

"Sup bro. How's ya girl?"

"Man I got a son kid!"

"Word? Me too dude!" Messiah smiled.

"Damn bro we got it in didn't we? Shit, congrats my nigga."

"Blessings to you too."

"Shit where you at?"

"Man, I'm on my way to the shop to pick up Red then I'm gonna drop her off and head to the crib. Why wassup?"

"Awe okay. Nothing shit I was just trying to see if you wanted to stop through and blow one wit' a nigga to celebrate, ya know."

"Oh. Man dude I'm on somethin' right now though. But I gotchu later though. Straight up."

Danger had to admit his feelings were kind of hurt. He knew his brother like the back of his hand and knew when he was getting the cold shoulder. Part of him knew that the reason had to have been that shit with Alexis but another part of him wanted to believe that Messiah had gotten over that by now.

They were not ones to hold grudges so he wondered why he was holding on to this one for dear life. He wanted to apologize to his brother for them millionth time. He wanted to explain to him that he tried so many times to break it off with her but she was so evil, so persistent, so controlling that he just could not seem to shake her. But he knew if he kept picking at that scab that eventually it would bleed.

"Well, yeah hit me later bro. I really wanna kick it wit' you man. Call me back." Danger begged sincerely.

"I gotchu."

As Messiah hung up the phone he stared down at the checkered pattern tile on the floor knowing that he wasn't going to call him back. Danger stuffed the phone back in his pocket then slowly headed back to the room to find Amy fast asleep and as quiet as a mouse. He pulled a near by wooden chair over to the bed and settled in. he was determined to stay by her side to be the first thing she saw when she unfastened her eyes.

"Amy, I know I haven't been the perfect man. I know that I've broken your heart and stumped on it a billion and one times. But I promise that I will start to do better from this day forth. Not just for you but for our son too." Danger lowered his head touching her hand with it caressing her skin with his. "I've been thinking about boy names. Maybe we could call him junior. You would like something like that, I figure."

Danger took a deep breath then stood and walked over to the window sticking his hands in his pockets. He stared out onto the neighborhood wondering if there were people out there making the same decisions he was. Most men wouldn't even be thinking about settling down with the one woman you had your child with and doing right by her. They would only be interested in taking care of the child, if that. He was determined not to be one of those men. Danger did not want his son to grow up to be a womanizing man whore, treating women like disposable objects. He wanted his son to grow up to be a fine distinguished gentleman that any woman would fight to be on his arm.

"Babe. I promise to love you forever. Nothing you can say or do will ever make me leave you. I'm sorry that it's taken me this long to come to my senses but I'm promising you that I'm going to be the man you want me to be. I'm gonna provide for my family and my wife doesn't have to do anything but spend money. Know that."

"Man. Where were you when I was going through my Latino phase?" The heavyset nurse said interrupting him and fixing her spiked up Mohawk.

"Ha ha, so you heard my confession huh?"

"Yeah. I gotta say it's a damn good one too. She's lucky to have such a good man." She said as she entered the room and headed to check Amy's machines.

"Hmm. I wasn't always a good man." Danger scratched his head softly. "Shit, if anything, I'm lucky to have her and my seed."

"Baby, none of that matters. You just proclaimed your undying love to her and she wasn't even listening. Then you vowed to do better when no one was around. That means that you are sincere. You weren't looking for validation and you weren't showboating for your boys. In my book, that means something." She said laying a nice warm heavy blanket on top of Amy and tucking her in nice and neat.

The nurse winked her eye twice at Danger before shimmying out of the room. He watched thinking that if he were his old self he would have banged that chunky nurse in a linen closet or bathroom somewhere, easy. She was throwing it at him while his girl lay helpless in front of them but she didn't care. If he were his old self, he would not have cared either. He would have put her on her knees and made her work for his affection. But the second that he thought of how he would make the nurse pay for her naughtiness, he looked down at Amy lying still below him and knew that it would not be worth it. Amy meant so much more than that.

"You gave me a beautiful son and now I'm going to make you my wife. There's no way I'm living without you." Danger recited as he took his seat right back at her side and kissed her hand. "I love you baby girl."

Chapter 13
Better Luck Next Time

Messiah walked in the door of the office startling Red. She wasn't paying attention to the door having been bored out of her mind all day. No one came into the office to purchase any units and after her minor scare earlier she had decided to kick her feet up and get some relaxation in. She looked at the time on the computer noticing it was almost 8pm and the sun had just about abandoned the sky. He stood waiting for her to log out without so much as a peep from either of them. Her facial expression read of tired and emotionally conflicted thoughts some of which Messiah was not Once she was done they each stepped outside while he locked up the office tight then released the shutter doors and set the alarm.

"So anyway I thought there was someone outside of the window stalking me and when I got out there with the piece to blast they ass, it turns out it was the damn bush. Isn't that funny?" Red said slapping Messiah on the arm.

"Yeah…funny." Messiah scratched the back of his head. "Ay, I just gotta run downstairs for a minute. Why don't you go sit in the truck? I'll only be a minute."

"No. I wanna go. I've done enough sitting for today don't you think?"

Messiah didn't find that quite funny at all. They hopped in the truck and headed down to the shop unit door. He had a very solemn and serious look on his face like he was thinking about something of great importance that he could not talk about. They exited the car simultaneously while he hit the button on his keypad allowing the door to rise. Once they were in, he returned the door to its closed position then entered the elevator and gone down.

"So, what you coming down here for?" Red asked knowing she was prying into his business rather rudely.

"If you must know, I'm thinking about keeping this place on the legit side. I'm tired of the game, ya know." Messiah responded as they headed down the semi-dark hallway gazing upon the tattered ruin of his multi-million dollar business.

"Are you serious right now?"

"As a heart attack."

"Okay, do you not know what you have here?" Red asked as he turned the key to his office door and flicked on the light as he entered.

"Red, I've been doing this for a long time now. There's nothing special about this place that I don't already know." He said as he shuffled through papers in his tall corner file cabinet.

"Then if you know there's something special here you need to keep this business going. You could be bigger than just this site. You can be bigger beyond your wildest dreams and I can help you."

"Oh yeah. Little big bad girl wants to help the old guy get his foot back in the door, huh? Well I ain't biting. There are things that you probably won't understand and besides I have my reasons." Messiah said taking a seat behind the desk.

"And what reasons are those? Your baby, your son? Your marriage or is it in fact Braze? What would make you want to throw your money away?" Red crossed her hands much like the vexed look on her face. "Messiah you can't give up now. Not now."

"And what are you getting out of this? Why do you want this so badly?"

"Because I believe in you baby. I believe that we can rock this city, maybe even this state or the country. I've only sat up there in that office one day but I've been working down here for a minute and I know that you can do better than this."

"And you're supposed to head all of this up, huh Red? Now just how are you supposed to do that?"

"With your help." Red said as she placed her fist knuckles down on his desk. "First of all we need to cop some high grade X. Not none of that busted stuff you've been selling."

"Wait, what? Baby, do you know what I've been selling out of here this whole time? That stuff is pure grade. None out here like it. Well of course except my supplier but we're the only ones who have it."

"Oh please! You call that mess top grade? I watched crack heads get higher than that on the street, Messiah."

"Woman you trippin'. Have you ever tried it?"

"No." Red replied softly as she walked over to the sofa taking a seat.

The truth was she had only seen how high Braze could get off of popping them in. She didn't want to blurt that out to Messiah and stir up his feelings especially if he didn't know. It wasn't her place to out that business even if the kid was involved. Red felt like since she had no time or desire to connect with the child she really didn't give a shit about it or its mother. Even though Messiah was supposedly the father she would only pretend to be the least bit concerned. Messiah reached down pulling open one of the drawers behind his desk then came up waving his arm towards her.

"Here. Try one, then."

"Messiah, now I know you trippin'. I ain't takin' that shit!" Red snapped.

"Well then how are you gonna bash my product when you know nothing about it?" He asked slamming the pink capsule down on the desk.

"Have you tried it?"

"Why wouldn't I have? It's my product. I need to know what I'm selling, right?"

"I don't know about that shit."

"What? You don't trust me? I'm not gonna slip you the date rape drug or nothing. Nobody is here but you and me. Look, if its any consolation, this isn't like cocaine or heroin. You can't become addicted."

"I know. I know what X does to people. I've just never tried it."

"I thought you would've done way worse than this, living on the streets and all." He laughed looking over into her unwavering eyes. "I mean, no offense."

"Anyway, whatever I did or didn't do on the streets it was all in the name of survival. You understand." She retorted shooting him devilish eyes.

"Whoa, whoa. Slow down chief. I don't want no trouble. I'm just saying you can trust me. I wouldn't do anything to hurt you." Messiah laughed throwing his hands up, surrendering. "Here, I'll take one and you take one. Deal?"

Red shook her head in agreement then moved in snatching the pink capsulated drug from the desk and popped it in her mouth quickly. She held it there hesitant to swallow it wondering if he was really going to swallow his or not. Messiah reached down in the drawer and came back up holding out his hand revealing the contents. He had two pills in his hand that he swiftly tossed in his mouth and swallowed with ease. Red went over to the silver colored mini-fridge in the corner reaching inside and pulling out a bottle of water then cracked it open tossing back her neck as she drank it.

Messiah stood taking the bottle from her hand then tossed back a few gulps himself before setting it down on the table. He snatched the top out of her hand and threw it on the desk never skipping a beat from his gaze into her big brown eyes. A warm sweet smell enveloped her nose and became stronger by the minute. Red licked her lips wanting to taste it desperately but she couldn't pinpoint where it was coming from. Her mind started to drift into his gaze listening to how peacefully quiet the room was. It irritated the shit out of her.

"So. Now what?"

"Now...we wait."

"I don't feel anything happening. I told you that this shit was a dud." Red laughed a little than covered her mouth as it became hysterical.

"Yeah. You don't feel nothing." Messiah stared.

"Nope. Absolutely nothing." She said as she slowly backed up feeling behind her for the sofa then taking a seat.

"Redina, If I touch your leg will you tell me to stop?" Messiah asked licking his thick full lips making them extra moist.

"Um, no. Why are you asking me that?" Red asked leaning back wiping the sweat droplets that were forming and dripping down the side of her face.

"Would you like it if I spread your legs apart and massaged your inner thighs?"

"Um…what?"

"What if I liked you from your toes all the way up to your perfectly plumped lips. Would you like that?"

"Messiah. Ooo, I like that name. Messiah. Mmmm. What are you doing to me?" red exclaimed breathing heavily as she ran her fingers slowly down her belly.

"Did I tell you to touch that?"

"No. But it's so hot in here. I'm so hot in here."

"You okay, Redina? Do you need me to come down there and cool you off?"

"How you gonna do that?"

"I could blow on you."

"Messiah, you are truly losing it." Red laughed unconscious to the fact that she was gyrating uncontrollably on his sofa.

He stood there watching her sway her body in all directions, much like a snake slithering cautiously on the ground. She looked like she was dancing on air with no restrictions and seemed to be enjoying her lighter than air moves from the smile planted on her face. Messiah loved the view. There was immediate growth in his pants that he didn't try to fight, allowing the bulge to poke out noticeably. Red was lost in her own world feeling the luxurious results of the X whether she knew it or not.

Messiah kneeled down in front of her using two fingers beginning at her left ankle and slowly moving up along her calf the up to her inner thigh. He watched as Red trembled loving every chill being sent through her body from his touch. She didn't even notice him remove her shoes and jogging pants even though all five of her senses were heightened to her very core.

"Mmmm. You taste so good." Messiah exhaled as he licked her calves one after the other then moved in for her juicy thick thighs. "So good."

The salty buttery taste of her skin filled his mouth like cotton candy from a carnival. He drooled, savoring every bit of her flavor, never wanting it to end. Red lifted her right leg in the air then let it rest on his wide strong back pointing her toes trying to be woman enough to withstand his inflicted pleasures. No one had ever touched her as gently as he had. No one had ever kissed her or caressed her as sensual as he. She was lost in his rhythmic translation of love.

"Stop teasing me." She breathed desiring more.

"Why? You don't feel anything. Remember?" He responded through licks.

Red smiled. Messiah looked up noticing just how beautiful it was. He removed his button down Oxford seductively revealing his bulging muscular pectorals right down to his near washboard abs. Red reached out to touch them but was batted away by his hand as he stood to rid his body of the lower half of clothing he adorned. Red reached around to remove her clothes but found herself once again being punished for her actions. He stood in front of her face stroking his manly tool, working it to get it brick style.

"Look at it." He demanded.

Red opened her eyes happy at the view. He was nice and chunky, not too big but big enough to do the job. She couldn't wait to get him inside of her. She wondered if he was looking for some sort of reassurance of his girth. For her, words could not express what she was feeling inside. After all, she had never had any real pleasure from sex. It was all always business with her and nothing more. But this time, she was going to be sure she made this one count as if she were a born again virgin.

She turned her body around propping up on her knees and quickly inserted his schlong into her mouth. Messiah didn't resist. He planted his massive hand on the top of her head and aided her motion as she bobbed back and forth releasing saliva to moisten the shaft. Her jaws locked around him sucking hard on the way up and licking with her tongue on the way down. She made a C shape with her hand placing it over his piece in front of her mouth then mimicked the motion back increasing her grip in a massaging form.

"Ahh, shit!" Messiah moaned deeply looking down at the art that Red was delivering to him.

It felt so good that he began pumping back into her mouth as if it were her pussy he was driving into. Red loved ever minute of it. She wanted him to abuse her mouth like she had been a very bad girl. She needed to be punished in every nasty way possible. She reached behind him grabbing his tight firm ass cheeks forcing him to ram hisself inside of her harder and harder. Messiah could hear the ganging noises she made every time his dick hit the back of her throat and began concerned.

He tried to pull out but her grip was immeasurably resilient. It wasn't until she began to slow down her movements that he realized he was trying to swallow his dick. He had never had that done before but it felt better than damn good. He felt himself climbing on a cloud higher than any he had ever seen making him want to scream so badly. His teeth tighten along with his face and eyes hoping she didn't make him bust before he wanted to.

Red released her sucking but went dead in again, coming all the way off of it allowing saliva to dance from her mouth to the tip of his shaft. She sucked it all up as she went back down onto him then released it again.

"Oh! Oh!" Messiah chanted as she sucked and licked his schlong to death.

"I want that shit." Red spat between sucks. "Give it to me. Right in my mouth."

"Damn, you nasty girl."

She looked up into his eyes smiling and laughing, never skipping a beat on his Johnson. It was there. Red would get her wish very soon. Messiah wanted to stop there was nothing he could do. He feared if he yanked out of her mouth she might accidentally scathe him with her teeth, which would have ended the night on a bad note. He jerked a few times then stood on his tippy toes shoving deeply inside of her no matter how badly she choked drowning the back of her throat with his seedlings.

"Arghhhh!" He bellowed squeezing her hair tightly. "My bad."

"It's cool." Red said removing hair from her eyes and straightening it back in place on her head, licking her lips profusely. "You taste so good."

Messiah heard his phone buzz off the hook but was uninterested in its caller. Red turned to sit down correctly with the look of disappointment on her face. He peeped her expression wondering what it was about but he didn't want to kill the mood with questions.

"Come here babe." He said holding out his hand to help her up.

He used his nails to tickle her sides as he removed her tank from over her head and then unhooked her bra forcing her ample breasts to bounce out greeting him with erect nipples. His mouth engulfed her round brown nipples as he flickered his tongue rapidly across her nipples sending a ripple of shockwaves through her body as she trembled. She wanted it bad as he moved from left to right on each tit. Once he freed himself from her enticing pair, he gently pushed her down on the sofa propping her legs in the air.

"Grab ya toes and never let them go."

Red was so excited that she could barely contain herself and catch her breath. She wanted to grab the back of his head much like he did her and make his face one with her pussy. She had never been able to sit back and enjoy some head without reservations. It was going to be a long awaited pleasure that she would definitely remember for years to come. Her first. She closed her eyes waiting for Messiah to mount his lips upon hers. A few minutes went by stroking her anticipation as she patiently waited for his move.

"Eh, what's wrong babe?" Red asked opening one eye to peek at what he was doing.

"Nothing. I'm good." Messiah panicked as he stroked his soft limp dick struggling to get it back at attention.

"Oh. Well, you know what baby its okay. I mean we can always do it some other time." Red sounded disappointed once again as she sat up looking for her clothes.

"Naw man. The first time we do it, it can't go down like this." Messiah shook his head as he plopped down on the sofa. "That's that shit she was talking about."

"Who?"

"Oh, uh, nobody." He placed his hand on her back to rubbing lightly. "I'm sorry baby."

"Hey you. It's okay, really." She assured him pausing from dressing giving him a peck to his lips. "Sex isn't everything. Sometimes it's just the connection you have with that person. I connect with you on so many levels that this one thing doesn't affect me." Red smiled.

Even though the words flowed from her mouth she was unsure if she actually believed them herself. She was fully dressed but Messiah sat there asshole naked on the sofa still wondering what the hell happened to the performance of his Johnson. He tried to remember if it had ever gotten like that with Braze or Zadie but his memory was a little hazy from the X.

"So, can I run the business or not?"

"Red!" Messiah snapped as he rose to look for his clothes.

"Don't do that Messiah. I wouldn't fuck you. You need to learn to trust somebody. Why not start with me?"

"Because my fucking brother has been trying to get this business for the longest and I tell him no all the time—"

"So we can do it together!"

"You obviously don't know Danger." Messiah buckled his pants. "He'll run this fucking place into the ground."

"Messiah, calm down. Your problem is that you don't trust people. If you are going to let it go you might as well give it to somebody who is going to do something with it."

"Woman, let's go. We'll discuss this in the morning."

"There ain't nothing to talk about. Its either yes or no."

"We'll see." Messiah said as he flicked the light switch.

Chapter 14
"I DON'T LOVE YOU!"— Red

"Man where the fuck you been, Meech. I've been blowing ya phone up crazy." Skid said walking around to the driver's side of the car. "Hey, Red."

"Wassup." Red replied as she leaned overplanting a sweet kiss on Messiah's cheek then exited the car swaying her hips towards the building.

"What's da deal?" Messiah said breaking Skid's trance from Red's booty.

"Man, why you ain't call me and tell me that shit man? You know you ain't call me cause ain't no missed call on my phone and shit."

"Skid what are you talking about?"

"Braze. You had me go pick that damn girl up from Christ and you didn't even bother to call me and tell me she was getting out or go pick her up or nothin'. I'm startin' to question the way you doin' business, man. Shit is unprofessional dude. Straight up."

"Wait a minute. Hol' up. Braze is out the hospital? She just had the baby today."

"That's what the fuck I said."

"This fucking girl done left the damn hospital. Where you take her to man?"

"That's the thing dude." Skid looked around at the darkness behind the complex noticing movement but unable to put his finger on exactly what it was. "I took her to your crib, man."

"YOU WHAT?"

"Man I tried to call you a million times. She said that you said take her there. I didn't know what the fuck was up man and you ain't answer yo phone." Skid explained.

Messiah put his head down on the steering wheel knowing that he was about to drive into the eye of the storm. His heart thumped fast as ever wondering what kind of turmoil awaited him back at his domain. Apart of him wanted to slap the shit out of Skid just for pulling some dumb shit like that but he knew he was easily swayed by the temptation of the flesh. Braze could have easily thrown the pussy at him knowing he would buckle and cave to her every command.

"Aight. I'm outta here. Watch her for me."

"Hold fast, dude. I need to holla at you about something man." Skid said placing his hands in the window.

"Skid, I don't have time for this shit right now dude."

"Well got damn it you need to make time cause this is some serious shit."

"Aight, we'll rap tomorrow. Just watch her."

"Yep." Skid sighed deeply as he backed up a little watching as Messiah drove like a clown on fire out of sight.

Even though her realized that Braze had gotten over on him, it made him chuckle to learn that Messiah was about to catch hell once he got home. He walked inside of the building wanting to stop by Red's apartment to talk to her about what had happened earlier that day but he didn't want to continuously freak her out about the situation. He leaned against her door trying to listen to see if he could tell what she was doing but all he heard was running water. *She must be getting in the shower.* He thought to himself licking his lips. *Damn.*

Red in fact was getting into the shower, having just dropped the last of her clothes onto the floor and stepped inside. She pulled the curtain and grabbed her loofah on a stick lathering up with her favorite ocean smelling body wash. She went down stroking in between her legs making sure to get all of the gooey wetness that she had exploded onto herself. Most of her thoughts centered on taking over the Candy Shop, the thought of that kind of power got her moist. Messiah obviously didn't care what kind of goldmine he had if he was willing to give it up because of his child. But Red was young, eager, and ready to take on all that the business had to offer.

"Arghhhh!!" She screamed loudly as she was yanked out of the shower by her curtain and by the shoulders. "Who are you? What the fuck do you want?"

The assailant didn't speak. He dragged her kicking and screaming into the bedroom and tossed her on the bed as if she were a simple piece of clothing. Red curled up on the bed covering herself with the torn clear shower curtain barely wrapped around her. She looked to the left and right of her at both coffee tables hoping to find something that she could use to stab with. Unfortunately for her, the darkness of the room blocked her line of sight. The only light available came from the bathroom down the hall.

"Don't even think about reaching for that phone." The assailant spoke in a deep raspy voice.

"What the fuck do you want?" Red asked stalling until she figured out a plan.

"You'll find out soon enough." The dark figure stood in the corner of the room watching her every move.

"Well, can I at least put some clothes on? Ugh."

The figure was silent. Red shook her head pissed that whoever this was trying to exact revenge on her for whatever reason didn't have to make her wait to die. She was impatient like that. The things that she did in her life she most definitely wasn't proud of but she figured when it was her time it would be quick and painless.

"Hey motherfucka if you want to kill me just fucking shoot me in the head already. I ain't got time for this shit. I done seen everything except Christ anyway." Red snapped.

A rattling at the window forced everyone's attention that way. A dark figure climbed through the ground floor window with ease. The large figure towered over Red darkening the bit of light that illuminated her body. He leaned onto the bed with his knuckles down breathing a heavy stench of vodka in her face. She leaned back to gain some sort of relief but it was no use. It quickly filled the room.

"Oh how I've missed you so, my dear sweet, Redina."

Red's eyes bucked and every hair on her body stood up like static cling. No matter how hard she tried, her mind would never forget that voice. He was not disguising his voice with a voice box like his dark counterpart in the corner. It was eerie to hear the voice she so desperately wanted to escape and thought she might not ever hear from again.

"What…are you doing here?" Red asked fighting back tears.

"You didn't actually think I was going to forget about you and let you go that easily did you?" Pet smiled as he forcefully grabbed her by the hair pulling her in for a forehead kiss.

"Don't you fucking touch me!" Red gritted through her teeth as she writhed to pull away.

"Oh, baby. Don't be that way. I thought you and me had something good. Shit, we talked about everything. Well I talked and you listened but I told you things that I've never told anyone else, ever." He said stroking the skin under her chin.

"How the hell did you find me?" Red asked finally escaping his grasp getting up from the bed and standing on the opposite side of it.

"Awe, you know better than that. But just in case you don't, you do remember your good friend Tina right?" He said nodding back to the figure in the corner.

"Whoa! Pet, what the fuck? What the fuck was the point in me wearing the mask and talking through this stupid thing if you was just gonna out me like that?" Tina snapped ripping the skullcap off of her head along with the box taped around her neck.

"Shut the fuck up and go wait in the living room and make sure no one disturbs the door. I'm going to have a little fun with my next baby's momma here." He retorted.

"If you touch me I swear to God I will — "

"You will what? Please tell me how you will punish me. Will you drive a knife through my tongue after I've licked your pussy dry? Will you bite my dick off after I've driven it through you anally? Ooo, please do tell."

"Uggggggghhhhhhhhh!"Red screamed feeling no one would hear her and it was totally pointless.

"Save the screaming. It won't help you. Not anymore."

"Just fucking kill me now. Just please fucking kill me now!"

"Now why would I do that? I love you, Red. Don't you understand that? I only came here to give you my seed and whisk you away with me."

"I'm not going anywhere with you."

"Oh, but I think you are. I've got a nice place all set up for us in hot Tamale Mexico. It's going to be beautiful." His eyes were crazily fixated upon her.

"You have got to be fucking shitting yourself if you think I'm going anywhere with you. You're a weak pathetic bastard who can only get off by raping women." Red snarled as she headed for the bedroom door.

Pet grabbed her arm throwing her back making her fall on the bed hard. He slammed the door closed and pulled out a long sharp butcher's knife and sub-compact G26 and pointed right at Red's head as he flicked on the light switch. Red sat on the bed frantically attempting to cover herself so he wouldn't be tempted to touch any part of her. She grabbed hold of the bright red comforter on the bed pulling it close to her body.

"No. Leave it. I want to see every inch, every part of you." Pet said as he moved in almost hunting his prey.

"Why are you doing this?" Red asked looking around for anything she could use as a weapon.

She focused in on everything around the room noticing even the smallest things. Everything in the room needed to be accounted for as she set her plan in motion. Pet neglected one lone fact about this meeting that was different from their last. She wasn't tied up and she was capable of fighting back. It would be a cold day in hell before she allowed his disgusting paws to grace her body ever again. She made a mental note about everything, from the picture frame of her on her birthday on the wall to his right to the cell phone on the nightstand to her left.

"I told you. I thought we had a connection and I can't stop thinking about you. I need you Red. I have to have you in my life."

"But you should want someone who wants you back, Pet. I don't want you and I don't love you." Red tried to remain calm but her anger sprouted through anyway. "I DON'T LOVE YOU!"

"You will learn." Pet's eyes lowered with starched anger shooting through them from her words.

He ripped the comforter from her clenched hands effortlessly dropping it on the floor. His knew hit the bed as he crawled over to her on the bed. Red scooted away backing back towards the metal headboard until she couldn't go anymore. His rat like nose touched her chin then moved about her body as he worked to sniff around taking in her scent. He stuck the knife back behind his back into his pants but secured the gun in his hand shoving it in between her legs and up to her pussy.

"How does that feel?" He asked tonguing her erect nipple. "Mmm, looks like you like it."

"I'm cold." She sneered rolling her eyes.

"Don't be snippy with me. You don't want to make daddy mad now do you?"

"Ugh…" Red stopped. "No…no I don't."

"What?"

"Well. If we are going to be together, then I guess you're right. I need to get used to loving you. So why not start now?"

"Don't be smart. I don't like it when you're smart." Pet reached back as far as he could then came back delivering a hefty smack to her chunky brown cheek.

"I'm not. I'm not being smart, Pet." Red huffed clenching her sore cheek staring back at him. "I'm trying to be real with you."

"Well stop it. Just don't say anything."

Pet leaned in attaching himself back onto her nipple again sucking away like a nine-month-old baby. He didn't close his eyes the entire time, fondling himself as he gazed into her eyes. All Red could think of was lighting a match to lighter fluid with his body in the midst of the flame. She couldn't bring herself to look down at him. She winced every time a shot of pleasure crept through her body. She tried her best not to like the feeling but it seemed the nerves in her body didn't resonate that memo. When he was done he reached up and slapped her again but not as hard as the last time. He figured it would keep her in line and keep her spirits low. She was to love him but not too much.

"Now, I want you to lay down and spread your legs and put your arms around me. Don't move, scream, or moan or I swear to God I will blow your fucking brains out." He grinned devilishly.

"But I thought you loved me?"

SLAP! SLAP!

Red was full of tears that wouldn't fall. She knew if she gave him the benefit of the doubt that it would only make him happy and then he would win the battle. He was not worthy enough to win neither the battle nor the war so she told herself to remain calm. All she needed to do was let him have his way with her yet again and let him think he had the upper hand. *Stupid motherfucka.* She thought repeatedly.

Chapter 15
Danger & Amy

Messiah sat in the car in front of his home wondering what the hell he had gotten himself into. This wasn't the first time he had to resolve an issue with two women facing each other but because of Braze's lack of regard for his space, he was sure it would not be the last. He needed to somehow get it through her head that he was not interested in having any kind of relationship with her now or ever. It was crazy to him that for some reason she couldn't get it through her head that just because they had a baby didn't mean that they needed to be together. The very fact that she was stuck on him bewildered him to his core anyway. He was a man who was intimately challenged in the bed and didn't understand her attraction to him besides his money. But he knew it went beyond that because she was borderline losing her mind over him.

He exited the car exhaling a deep breath slowly and fiddling with his keys. The lights were on in the living room so he knew that either Braze was still there and they were having drinks and a male bashing party or one of them had killed the other and the surviving one was trying to figure out what to do with the body. As he approached the door and turned the key, the noises eroding from inside plagued his being.

"Hello?" He said softly knowing no one would hear him.

His foot steps were as silent as his voice as he attempted to tip toe his way up the stairs to retrieve some clothes and head back out. He made it to one of the stairs before hearing the noises again and they were coming from the kitchen. It was hard to ignore them because it was something he so very rarely heard especially in his household. Against his better judgment, he crept down the hallway and into the kitchen but only peeked his head in trying to see what was going on.

"Who the hell is that?" Alexis shouted grabbing a long pitchfork from the dish block on the marble island counter.

"Whoa! Whoa! It's just me." Messiah said busting in putting his hands up.

"Oh! Baby, you scared the shit out of me."

"Yeah, I could say the same thing." He retorted. "What's uh, what's going on?"

"Well baby, you forgot to tell me that your sister was coming to visit. And look at me I was in my nighty and heels trying to be sexy for you and you didn't tell me we had company coming." Alexis rambled on with a freakish wide smile. "And guess what? I cooked!"

"Oh you did?" Messiah laughed curiously. "My sister, eh."

"Yeah silly. But you got here too late, babe. We done ate and everything. Now we sitting here catching up and drinking wine." Alexis said taking another sip of chilled Pinot Grigio from her glass.

"So, sis, where's the baby?" Messiah turned to ask Braze with a raised eyebrow.

"He's upstairs fast asleep in the guest room, big bro." Braze squinted her eyes as she took a sip from her glass.

"Well, I told them they didn't have to spend money on a hotel, they could just stay here. I mean, what's the point in having this big ol' house if we can't share it with nobody, right?" Alexis interjected.

"Most definitely, my wife. Most definitely." Messiah turned to leave.

"Wait Messiah. Don't you wanna sit and have a few laughs with us? Maybe even a drink or two?" Alexis walked over caressing his chiseled arm.

"Naw. Think I'll leave you two to it. Gonna go upstairs and see my *nephew* and take a shower." He cut his eyes back to Braze.

Braze sat there immersed in the performance he put on in front of her. Well done. She though in her mind loving the fact that Messiah chose not to cause a scene. Alexis had filled her in on all of the happenings and even included the fact that she had lost her memory and was desperately trying to fix her marriage. It was magical finally being able to be in Messiah's beautiful house and feeling a small taste of what it would be like to be her. Alexis watched as Messiah left the room feeling a bit disappointed that he was not in mood to entertain guests.

"Well, I guess it's just you and me tonight girl." Alexis said returning to her glass downing it in one gulp. "Maybe he'll kick it with us tomorrow."

"Awe girl we don't need him to have fun." Braze said continuously filling Alexis' glass with more wine. "You just drink up and have a ball."

The two women laughed so loudly that it could be heard all the way upstairs in the guest room where Messiah was viewing his son. He was in the middle of the huge fluffy white spread on the bed fast asleep. He shook his head in disbelief that he had chosen a mother

like Braze for him. He wished that he were thinking more with the head sitting above his shoulders rather than the one in between his legs when he so carelessly inserted his seed into her womb. His hand gently grazed the bottom of MJ's foot as he walked out of the room allowing the baby to get the rest he so deserved.
****

Amy awoke groggy and staring into Danger's face with his head leaning back on the chair snoring as loud as a wilder beast. She looked around the room then down at her belly slowly remembering everything that had happened. It was all coming back to her as she remembered the very last thing that was said before she drifted off to never never land. *The baby is alive.* Her only thoughts were not to see it. There was no way she was about to bond with a child she never wanted in the first place.

Danger had what he wanted. She stared at the curtain thinking of a way to get out from up under his hold. Even if she was to remain in the relationship with him she knew she would never be happy. He would have everything he desired and she would be living a complete lie. He would be living his dream life and she would be sitting in a corner regretting every minute of the day that she stayed with him. *The bridge is over.* She thought. Her heart thumped a mile a minute as she wondered how the hell she would get out of this mess with him without any consequences.

He stirred in his chair switching sides, moving from left to right. Amy laid her head back down on the pillow, closed her eyes, and slowed her breathing just in case he woke up to check on her. She was not in the mood for random conversation about the child he loved so dearly. It wasn't in her plan to reconnect with him or build a connection with her own flesh and blood. Danger began snoring again and scratching his ass as he fidgeted.

Amy's breathing returned to an erratic state as she slowly pulled the IV needle from her right arm. She used a piece of tissue on the table next to her to aid in her need to stop any bleeding that might have occurred. She scooted to the edge of the bed with a streak of dark red blood following behind her. Quietly her body cringed as she attempted to gradually open the closet door to find her clothes and something to plug up her pussy. The only clothes she found was the bloody maxi dress that she wore to the hospital and her flats. She slid the dress and shoes on without care then shut the closet door and turned around.

"Where you going, A?" Danger whispered faintly interlocking his fingers.

"Uh, I…"

"Why do you keep doing this to us? I provide for you, give you a loving family and home and this is how I get repaid?" He said thumbing a sniffing his nose simultaneously.

"D., we haven't been happy for a long time and you cheating didn't help. Don't act like you didn't know." Amy panicked.

She still loved him and still had that fear of leaving him to his face but her mind was made up. There was no more effort being put into their relationship. There was only the baby and it was not enough for her to want to keep going through his womanizing sexist ways.

"I thought we were going to work this out. I mean we got the baby and everything. I just knew we were going to make it."

"Can I still work? Will you honestly be okay with me being a working mother?"

"Amy, we talked about this shit man—"

"Will you?"

Danger pouted as he lowered his head trying to gain his composure. The one thing that the both of them did have in common was the fact that neither of them liked public spectacles.

"Amy if this is about that shit that happened earlier, babe, you gotta know that I never meant to hurt you."

"You always never mean to do something, D. You never mean to slip and fall into pussy, you never meant to bust inside of me all those times, oh my personal favorite, you never meant to give me an STD." Amy placed her hands over her face massaging roughly to relieve stress. "It's over, D."

"Amy—"

"No! It's over. We can't keep living a lie. We just can't."

"But what about our son? He needs a family, Amy. We deserve to give him that much. He's innocent in all this." Danger stood as she backed away.

"So give him one then."

"Huh?" Danger queried confusingly.

"Ugh, look D. I can't take care of a baby. There's no way that I would be able to hold on to a baby and care for it while I'm out doing the work that I love." Amy sighed.

"So you would choose your work over your own flesh and blood?"

"The truth is, I never developed a bond with the kid. Even when I felt it—"

"Him…when you felt *him* inside of you."

"Okay, Danger. When I felt *him* inside of me, I couldn't form a connection to him. I just wanted this pregnancy to be over so I could get back to being me. To a normal life." Amy went over to warm his cheek with the back of her hand soothingly.

"How could you bear a life from your flesh and then say something like that?"

"You say it like it's a bad thing. Look you wanted this baby, I could've easily gotten an abortion. I told you I wasn't ready." Amy bellowed nervously, cutting her eyes at him. "You pressured me to keep it."

"Him! And don't try and turn this around on me. This ain't about me. This is about you wanting to be selfish and choose your career over your priorities." Danger retorted.

"I don't have time for this and you are not about to argue with me about this. I'm leaving and that's that. You can have the kid I won't even fight you for him. I don't even want my name on the birth certificate." Amy walked over to the door with her heart beating faster than ever. It was a major adrenaline rush for her to be taking a stand and finally thinking about her feelings and no one else's.

"Amy if you walk out that door I never wanna see your face anywhere in Chicago again." Danger threatened hoping to place some fear in her heart.

"That's fair." She agreed.

"I might be forced to deal with you on a bloody level if I did." He added piercing his eyes through the back of her head.

Amy smirked and turned slightly. She peeled her eyes from the floor planting them dauntingly upon Danger's face. It read genuine, displaying no lies. Amy's expression went from concerned to business in ten seconds. Her smirked mutated into a full-fledged eerie looking ear-to-ear smile.

"Bring it on then." She cooed as she turned walking out the hospital room door and disappearing into the night.

Danger turned around taking a seat and with a deep sigh interlocked his fingers. Although he acted hard in front of her, he heart was a bleeding sea of jilted emotions. So much was happening so fast, it was too much to bear. But one thing was certain, there was no way he could be a killer and still take care of his son without fear of getting done and leaving him parentless. Being a father was more important than all of that stupid street running he did and since he was a single parent his child would always have to come first. He took his phone out of his pocket and dialed a number he knew he might regret later but right now it was the best thing.

"Hey bro." Danger sighed. "I am calling to let you know that I won't be able to do this no more man. I can't work the streets for you no more and I can't handle business. Amy's gone and it's just me and the baby. I gotta do it right for my little man, ya know. You might not hear from me for a while cause I'm gonna be focusing on the baby and when he gets better we gonna be moving, far away. Some place where we can have a normal life. You know I'm not gonna answer your call backs because you're gonna try and talk me out of it. I love you bro but I'm a family man now."

Beep.

Chapter 16
"That info that you need."—Skid

Tap! Tap! Tap!

"Red? I heard some noises from all the way upstairs and I'm just coming to check in on you." Skid said turning the knob and entering her apartment without invitation.

"Yeah. I'm fine, now leave." Tina responded disguising her voice in a high-pitched fashion before kneeling down behind the kitchen island.

Skid's eyebrow raised, suspiciously knowing that Red was acting really strangely even for her. He walked in looking towards the kitchen wondering where the hell was she or even if the voice had come from there. His huge footsteps were silent on the carpet as he headed towards the kitchen turning the corner of the squared opening. He looked down to see a kneeling Tina crouched down in front of the dishwasher.

"Take that fucking mask off before I spread your brains all over that wall." Skid demanded as he pulled his gun out from behind his back.

"You don't understand. I'm just here to protect Red." Tina lied and stood as she lifted the skullcap off of her head revealing two black eyes.

"You? Bitch you better start talking." Skid raised the gun all the way up pointing it to her head.

"Fuck you!" She yelled.

"Bitch," he cocked the gun then returned it to her head. "talk!"

Tina held her ground. She didn't want to give him any information and risk another beating from Pet. She after all was his little sister and had been in a relationship with him since they were kids. He possessed her, having some kind of hold over her that she could not seem to break. Rather than fight him, she just stuck with him allowing him to manipulate her and use her for his own selfish bidding.

"Man, I don't hit bitches but if you need me to knock out your two front teeth then so be it." Skid said raising the gun high up in the air forcing it down as Tina covered her face with both arms.

"Ok! Just don't fucking hit me no more." Tina screeched.

"No more? Bitch I ain't hit you yet. Now I ain't got time to be fucking playing wit' you. Where's Red?" Skid's teeth were clenched together showing pissed off disgusted demeanor.

Tina pointed towards the back in the direction of the bedroom, crying as she slowly squated down to the floor balling like an injured dog in the street. Skid backed up never resting his arm or lifting an eye from Tina, as he went to nigga-rig the door so she could not weasel her way up out of the apartment. He then made his way police like down the hallway and up to the room door. Skid placed his hand on the door to see if it would push open but when it didn't he knew once he turned that knob it would be on with whomever was on the other side of that door.

"Red? You in there, baby?" Skid yelled placing his back firmly up against the wall.

CLICK! BOOM!

A single shot was fired at the door blasting a whole through it forcing particles of shattered wood to fly in various directions. Most of it hit Skid in his face, arms, and stomach. He checked hisself to see if he was okay. There ere a few pieces of splinter like wood lodged in his skin but nothing he couldn't handle. He kissed his hand and thanked God that it wasn't a bullet that hit him then turned his defense mode back on. He wanted to peek through the hole but felt it unsafe to do so.

Crash!

Skid turned and jolted the room door open with one powerful kick then when in ready to blaze the motherfucka that tried to get him.

"AGGHH!"

The pulsating screech of Red's voice resonated through the apartment walls and the bodies of everyone in its path. She moved quickly to pull the huge knife out of Pet's pants and drive it straight down into the small of his back. Her hands wiggled a little to remove the knife then plunged it right back down into him only higher up. Pet let out a faint moan and then only breathing and gurgling could be heard as she dug into him again and again and again. Blood shot out splattering on the walls and the floors until Skid ran over grabbing her arms to cease her brutal assault.

"Let me go! Let me go! This son of a bitch needs to die tonight!" Red screamed with a stream of tears flowing down moistening her cheeks.

"NO! Let him go. You betta than that shit, girl."

"Fuck that! I wanna slash his fucking throat!

"Naw, no you don't. I got something better planned for this nigga." Skid said as Pet rolled onto the floor. "Did he hurt you?"

"Naw. Son of a bitch was sucking on my titties and shit trying to make love with his bitch ass." Red howled launching a huge glob of spit from out of her mouth onto Pet's face.

They watched as he moaned for death and Tina returned to the bedroom covering her hands. She kneeled down at her brother's side praying over his body. Deep down inside she was meekly happy that he was not able to jump up and hurt her anymore but still he was her brother and long time lover. She hated to see him hurt and bleeding to no end. She wiped the blood from his arm amazed that he was even still alive with the amount of blood that he was losing.

"What now?" Tina asked shedding a few tears.

"Now we get this motherfucka outta here and we clean up this mess." Skid said releasing.

"I say we bury the motherfucka." Red responded as she tried to calm herself down from her murderous rage.

"No. I got something else in mind, but we need to move now. Red I need you to get up and put some clothes on baby. You get the fuck up and help me roll this motherfucka up in this blanket." Skid demanded.

"No...No I'm not helping you dump my brother." Tina cried.

"Your brother?" Red and Skid asked in confusing unison.

"Yeah. He's my fucking brother."

"Well it don't matter cause after we done with him, you next." Skid snapped as he whisked the bedspread off the bed and laid it across Pet's body. "Now grab a fucking end."

Tina began to shriek at the very thought. She was about to help them dispose of the only family she had ever known only to be tossed out like trash herself. Red looked at how meek and helpless she was and instantly felt remorse for her. She felt as though she was just a victim of Pet just like she was; only she was a long time victim. As she slipped on her jeans and gym shoes she began to realize that killing her would only be heartless. But with Skid's take charge attitude she knew arguing with him about that now wouldn't go over so well.

"Alright, pick this motherfucka up and carry him to my truck in the parking lot. Let's go!" Skid barked.

Red reached over to help Tina pick up Pet from the shoulders of the blanket. The women looked at each other wondering what the unspoken bond was they saw in each other. Skid was not the least bit entertained by it. He was used to fixing messes and this was one that needed to get done pronto.

"Um, y'all need to fucking move faster than this. We still gotta clean up this room." He said as they took baby steps out of the door careful not leave a bloody trail.

Once Pet was secure in the truck, Skid looked around for nosey neighbors or passersby but the coast was clear. He took out a Newport 100 from his pocket and blazed it up staring at Red becoming even more heavily infatuated with the fiery bombshell she was inside. It didn't come out often but he knew with him she could be the person she wanted to be 24/7 without the need for the good girl façade. He liked her just as feisty as she wanted to be and Messiah was only forcing that phony shit upon her because that's how he was.

"Aight, Red go lock up. You, get your ass in the truck and no funny shit or I swear I'mma plant two in ya dome. Ya dig?" Skid spat taking a puff of his square one last time before flicking it into the street.

Red did as she was told then ran back to the truck and hopped in. "Um, so what we gonna do?"

"Don't worry about that. Just know that wherever we go, you need to keep your mouth closed cause one wrong move could cost all of us our lives. You feel me on this?" Skid looked over at her grabbing her hand.

"Yeah. Yeah." Red answered feeling a change in Skid's demeanor towards her.

She knew it was about the kiss and hoped that he wasn't feeling her like that. It was not that he was ugly or anything but he was a little older than her taste preferred. Though she had to admit that his take-charge attitude did turn her on a bit, her heart remained true to Messiah. Tina sat in the back seat the whole ride on the expressway quite as a church mouse but keeping her eye on all of her surroundings. She was a master of getaways so she kept her eye out for any potential good one that would not cause her to be ducking and dodging for her life. There was no saving Pet but the first chance she got she was snatching a gun and protecting herself.

As they turned down a clean dark alley, Tina's heart began to pump times ten. Skid pulled up along the same long black gate that he did before but this time it just opened up automatically. He maneuvered the truck around backing it in then immediately cutting the ignition off. He reached into the glove compartment realizing that he had used that money to pay earlier.

"Red look up under your seat and give me that lock box." He asked softly.

"Where the fuck are we? This where y'all gonna kill me at?" Tina panicked looking around at the men approaching the car with big ass guns and facemasks.

"Didn't I say shut the fuck up?" He responded.

Red handed him the box. He unlocked it with a key hanging from around his neck and opened it up revealing stacks of large crisp bills. His colossal sized hands took out five of those stacks and locked the rest away tossing the box under his seat. Red watched his every move wondering just where the hell they were herself but she knew better than to ask questions. She trusted that Skid would never do anything to put her in harms way as she sighed heavily when they exited the car. The bright light that was shining down into the yard quickly faded away to darkness.

"Where? Where?" A Mexican refugee asked poking Skid with the end point of his machine gun.

"In the back." Skid pointed as another man escorted them inside.

They walked through darkness, Red felt around for Skid's hand and when she found it he squeezed her back so tightly she thought it was going to fall off. It sent chills up her spine then back down again as they neared what seemed like a big black hole in the middle of a room. The other men came in behind them pushing them to the side as the dumped Pet's body on the ground. The Stew Maker was in the corner puffing on some type of sweet smelling elongated cigarette.

"What is this? Who ordered this?" She asked moving in close to them.

Skid pushed Red behind him. "I ordered it. Here's your dough."

She signaled for her minion in the corner to take the money from him and count it. He thumbed it then gave the Stew Maker the okay eye. She looked around on her table of knives, pitchforks, icepicks, and large needles trying to decipher which one she would start with first. A moaning noise startled them all while the noticed that it was coming from the wrapped blanket.

"Oh he's not dead, eh?" The Stew Maker asked angrily.

"I thought he was."

"You thought wrong, eh?

"Oh and I need you to take this bitch right here too. If you want me to take her out there and kill her, I'll drop her." He said grabbing Tina by the arm.

"No…what the fuck?" Tina cried.

"That won't be necessary. We can tape their mouths." The Stew Maker smiled.

"Wait, Skid. I think we should let her go." Red interjected.

"What? Red, she's just gonna come and get revenge on you for her fucking brother." Skid retorted.

"No, I won't."

"See, she said she won't and even if she does…I'll be ready for her." Red replied demonically.

Skid looked into her eyes and knew she meant business. He released her letting her fly back against the muddy wall. Tina was relieved that she wasn't about to die a bloody gruesome death unlike her sibling lying a few feet from her. She figured it payback for the years of torture and trauma he had put everyone through whom he encountered, especially her. Her bond was broken and she was ready to move on with what was left of her life.

"What is this?" The Stew Maker grew impatient.

"Not her. Sorry for the inconvenience. We out, right now."

The Stew Maker shooed them away quickly and signaled for her minions to make sure they got out swiftly. They journeyed back to the truck and waited for the gate to open. Once they were out of the gate and at the end of the alley where traffic emerged, Red and Skid looked at each other simultaneously.

"Ay, you gots to get out." Skid said thumbing back to Tina.

"But know that if you come near me again, I will have your ass, Tina. It's not a game." Red warned.

"Bitch, I never wanna see your face again." Tina said as she quickly open the back door and closed it as she bolted down the street and around the corner.

"You think she'll come back for me?" Red asked turning to Skid as he drove off back towards the expressway.

"Naw." Skid said grabbing her hand, gently kissing her soft skin. "That bitch ain't crazy."

It was just what she needed to hear. Though it felt weird that he was touching her in a tender way, she knew he made her feel complete. He brought out the fighter in her. The one person she felt like she had been missing all this time with Messiah back in her picture. Skid made her feel like her old self and that was one thing she had tapped back into and was not willing to sacrifice anymore.

"Skid, you know me and Messiah — "

"You and Messiah, what?" Skid asked irritably. "I ain't one of them kats that just hang on females, Red. But I see something in you and I know we can be good together. That nigga's playing you. Straight up."

"How do you know that, Skid? He says—"

"You know what, I see you the type that never trusts nobody's information but your own. See, I like that about you. So let's go get it then."

"Get what?" Red asked inquisitively.

"That info that you need." Skid replied never taking his eyes off the road.

Chapter 17
"Don't cry for that nigga. He ain't worth it."—Skid

Messiah wrapped the towel around his waist tightly before leaving the bathroom and heading down the hall to his bedroom. He had reservations about going to sleep in that room but he blew them off knowing that he would just shut Alexis down if she tried any funny business. He found a pair of navy blue cotton briefs that he slid on along with an all white tank top. He hoped that he could hear the baby since the two cackling birds downstairs were drunker than ever and probably wouldn't. He lied back on the bed staring up at the ceiling contemplating how he was going to get both of those women out of his house and out of his hair for good.

"Awe! A sweet bed to lie in." Alexis said coming in the room dancing her way to the bed then plopping down next to Messiah.

"You're drunk. You should calm down before you wake up the baby." Messiah snarled as he turned over not wanting to smell any of the libations spewing from her breath.

"Baby. Can we talk?"

"What?"

"I just think that whoever I was before, I shouldn't be punished for that because I'm not that person now and I love you. I wanna make this work between us." Alexis said releasing miniscule burbs under each word.

"We've been over this, Alexis."

"Yes, yes I know. I was just saying, did we ever try to work on our marriage?" She asked biting her nails and turning to face his back. "I know I would like to try."

Messiah sighed heavily and closed his eyes before he spoke. "I don't think that's a good idea, especially right now."

"Why not though?" Alexis asked as she began caressing and softly pecking her kisses on his burly back.

"Because when you get your memory back you're just going to be back to your old self. I can't deal with that."

"What if I promise you that I won't be an asshole once I get my memory back?"

"Stop. Stop it Alexis."

She began to cry placing her hands over her face to shield Messiah's gaze. He rose from the bed pacing around the room. He started to think that he should've never opened his house up to her after he explained their situation. Instead he should've offered to pay for her hotel stay until she got her memory back or until the divorce was finalized, whichever came first. Now she was bawling like crazy on the bed and that was something he was never prepared for.

"Alexis, stop crying. I didn't mean to hurt your feelings."

"No I get it. We're over and I need to accept that. Sorry. If it's all the same to you I think I'll move out in the morning. I think I need to distance myself from you in order to get over you."

"Ugh, you don't have to move out. We just need to learn some boundaries. I want us to end this on a friendlier note." He said sitting down next to her.

"Friendlier, huh? Well somehow my life as been reduced to this all in one day." She responded as she began to cry into her hands again.

Messiah leaned over pulling her into his chest allowing her to cry her tears onto his shirt. He figured there was need for being mean and the more cordial they are to each other the better the divorce would be. He just could not get those papers soon enough in his eyes.

"Are we good here?" He asked giving her the puppy dog eyes.

"You're so cute." Alexis laughed. "Yes we're good."

"Okay, great. I'm gonna go check on the baby." Messiah laughed as he slapped her leg playfully then left the room.

He walked down the hall to the first guest room hearing the sound of singing the closer he became to it. Braze was in there singing some sort of lullaby to the baby. Messiah opened the door and walked over to the baby who was still fast asleep. It disappointed him a little because he wanted to play with the baby for a while before he went to bed. Braze stared up at him still singing and smiling into his adoring face.

"He looks like you, ya know." She said rising from the bed and walking up to him.

"Yeah, I know." He peeped her game quickly and removed her hands from his waist. "Braze, what are you doing?"

"Taking care of my man. You want a massage baby or do you want some head? There are plenty of things we can do until I heal in a few weeks." She said tugging at his boxers. " Shit I even know chicks that go back to fucking once they quit bleeding. I think it takes like a week or so."

"Don't you see me fighting you for a reason?"

"So stop it. Nigga you know you want me. Quit playing. Ain't no other bitch gonna love you like I love you and I got your fucking seed. Quit playing yourself." Braze responded forcefully and successfully pulling his boxers down and dropping to her knees.

Braze got to work doing his piece just the way he liked it. She squeezed his head and thumbed it gently as she smacked his head with her tongue. Messiah became like putty in her hands just from that move alone. Once she realized she had him she began sucking the tip and stroking his shaft. He had begun breathing heavily and moaning excessively loving the way she worked her magic on him. There was no denying that she was right. There was no other woman that would do him like she did.

"What the fuck is going on in here? Is that what you do, fucking your sister?" Alexis asked walking in the room bewildered.

"Are you really that naïve? Duh, I'm not his sister. I'm his baby's momma. His woman. His bitch. He's mine Alexis." Braze said going back to work. "He's always been mine."

"Ugh! What did I do to deserve this, Messiah?" Alexis asked crossing her arms.

But he couldn't speak. He was lost in the feeling that Braze's mouth delivered. Alexis' anger didn't really bother him, figuring it was a good way to keep her from trying to get back together. If anything, he would rather mess around with Braze because she was in his life for good no matter how hard he tried to fight it.

"His bitch huh? I'll show you who's his bitch." Alexis snapped back grabbing Messiah's face planting a sloppy wet tongue lashing on him.

"No. Lex…" Messiah attempted to fight but his loins wouldn't allow him to do so to well.

"Shut up!" Alexis bellowed sticking her tongue in his mouth.

While Braze did her thing down below, Alexis made sure she handled business up top licking and suck on Messiah's nipples while he fingered her hot wet snatch. He was unable to fight the tingling sensations shooting through his body, feeling as though he wanted to cum so badly. Alexis brushed her D-cups up on his broad chest then propped her leg up on the bed to give him a better feel, moaning excessively with her head tilted backward.

Outside, Red and Skid pulled up quietly in front of Messiah's house. She felt confused for second, not wanting to be there. Skid placed the car in park never cutting it off then taking a single key off of the ring on the set in the ignition. He took it and handed it to her with a blank face never uttering a word.

"What do you want me to do with this?" She raised her eyebrow refusing to take the key pushing his hand away.

"Let's see how good you are. Go get your information without being found and meet me back here in eight minutes."

"Huh? Are you crazy? I ain't going up in that man's house and it's dark in there too. Uh un, what if he catches me?"

"I thought you was a G."

"I am." Red replied rolling her head.

"Then you won't get caught. Gone and get your info, killa." Skid smiled as he handed the key back over to her.

Red didn't want to look like a punk even though she didn't want to do it. She thought that if Messiah was still banging his wife or other hoes she really didn't want to know about it. Reluctantly, she took the key and exited the car. The closer she got to the front door the faster her adrenaline rushed anticipating what evidence she might find inside.

The key turned with ease and silence prompting her to push the door open in the same structure. She stepped in and was immediately met with the sound of straight fucking going on upstairs. Her heart dropped recognizing the deep sultry moan from anywhere. It had only been a couple of hours since she last heard it.

She had to admit that hearing him being pleasured by someone other than her kicked a hole in her heart. Her feet crept up the stairwell but her mind was still stuck at the front door. Nothing could prepare her for the scene her eyes was about to witness.

"Ooo shit! Ride this dick baby!" Messiah moaned.

"Here, taste this pussy baby." Alexis said mounting his lips planting her ass right on his nose.

Red stood in the doorway as visible as could be. She didn't even attempt to hide secretly wanting all of them to see her in dismay at the door. Her palms became sweaty and her knees weak as she watched the threesome on the floor escalate. They were all moaning so loudly it amazed her that the innocent soul napping on the bed never flinched an inch. Messiah seemed to stay hard and strong with no five minute hiccups and was even banging back into Braze's bloody pussy.

It was all Red could do not to blow chunks right on hallway floor. Tears flowed from her eyes as she ran back down the stairs and out the door slamming the door behind her. It didn't matter if they heard her or not anymore. She ran right up to Skid's truck and jumped in releasing an ugly torrent of sorrow.

"Why did you bring me here?" She cried as she slammed the key down in his waiting hand.

"Don't cry for that nigga. He ain't worth it." Skid sighed. He didn't mean to make her cry, he just figured she had a right to know that Messiah wasn't the goody two shoes that he portrayed himself to be. "Hey listen, I didn't want to hurt you."

"How did you know he was in their fucking them?" Red asked trying to regain her composure.

"Actually, I didn't know that they were in there doing that. I just knew that a man in a house with two women who were obsessed with him wasn't gonna mix."

"No you knew. You had to know."

"I didn't know, Red. All I knew was that they were there." Skid side eyed her wondering why her heart was so heavy for Messiah. "Ay, did you fuck him?"

"That's none of your damn business." Red was pissed he would even ask her that.

"So you did huh?" Skid asked feeling the blood boiled over in his neck.

"Even if I did what's it to you? We aren't together and we never will be. I don't fuck friends."

"I'm not his friend." Skid boiled over driving like he was racing for Nascar.

Back in front of their building, Red quickly exited the car slamming the door in anger and running inside. She couldn't stop her tears from falling and she didn't want him to see her so hurt. Skid got out still pissed but knew he had to make it right with her.

"Awe, the man of the hour. Just the person I wanted to see." Haggley said stepping out of his pitch black Lincoln Town car.

"Shit." Skid lowered his head. "Man I'm all on it. I just need more time."

"You see, now communication is the key to any successful relationship." Haggley staggered over facing him. "So why haven't you answered any of my calls?"

"Been busy."

"Oh yes, busy. Yes, I know all about your skirt chasing endeavors." Haggley lied. "But I'm not interested in knowing what the head in your pants is thinking. Where's my boy?"

"I said I'm on it."

"Well I hope so. Cause the big fellas are becoming impatient. They want to do this very clean and dirty at the same time. But they won't wait forever." Haggley winked as he walked back towards his car. "You got 24 hours or the deal is off and we kill you and your big booty friend in there.

"Man, fuck man." Skid bellowed once the crooked cop pulled off.

Messiah had evaded them long enough and now they were using him to extract cold-blooded revenge. He wasn't feeling the fact they were using him but he knew he could use the money to funds a beautiful life with Red. Especially since he had just spent almost half of his fifty thousand dollar savings paying the Stew Maker. He never asked Messiah for any money back on his jobs figuring he had him, but Messiah never once offered to repay a penny. It was known that Skid had become too complacent as the right hand man and was never going to get the promotion or wage he so greatly desired.

Chapter 18
Like Butter

Skid walked in the building knowing what he had to do. He knocked on the door repeatedly but Red didn't answer. Behind the door, sobbing and running water could be heard echoing through the apartment. His colossal sized hand tried the knob but this time it was deadlocked shut. Skid lowered his head letting out a deep sigh knowing he had to get inside to talk to her no matter how mad she was with him.

"Red. Red I need to talk to you baby."

"Go away!"

"Red. I need to help you get that up now. There's a certain way that needs to be done. I don't want you to ruin it." Skid yelled through the door, hearing the sobbing end. "Come on baby. I gotta help you."

"Ugh! Help me with this shit then get the fuck out! I don't wanna talk and I for damn sure don't wanna hear what you gotta say."

"Got damn it, Red! Just listen to me." He said grabbing her by her the arms shaking her a bit. "I didn't take you over there to hurt you. I took you over there to show you that you deserve better than some wishy washy ass nigga that don't know what he wants and only has a back bone when its something that affects him."

"Why do you care so much about what the fuck I do, Skid? I'm nobody. I—"

"Because I think I'm in love with you, Red!"

Silence filled the air as the two stood staring into each other's eyes processing Skid's last words. Red didn't know what to make of what he had just said. It was almost as if she was living in some parallel universe. She forced her way free from his strong hold never taking her eyes off of him but now they held a puzzling look.

"What do you mean you think you're in...in love with me?"

Skid sighed closing his eyes and when he opened them again he realized that she was the most beautiful girl he had ever seen. None of the women he had ever encountered ever amounted to the type of woman she was. She was bad in the sense that she withstood anything a motherfucka threw at her. She was bold, making sure she said what was on her mind without reservation of what the next dude had to say and she was also dangerous. Red was never afraid to give a motherfucka that shit they deserved.

"I don't think. I know I love you. It might sudden for you but over these past few months I've just been sitting back and watching shit. I just watch in the cut and keep my mouth shut but baby, I know I can make you happy. I watched you chase a dream and when you said you was gonna leave him that was the best thing I had heard all day."

"Shut up Skid."

"I think that together we can be the Bonnie and Clyde of this bitch. You know? I need you just as much as you need me."

"Shut the fuck up Skid!"

Skid waited for her to say something, anything as he stood seemingly out of breath and breathing heavily. He wiped the sweat from his forehead nervously. It was the first time he had ever put his heart on his sleeve for a chick. One of whom he hadn't the foggiest idea of whether or not she felt the same way about him. Red put her hands on her hips still pondering and processing. Finally after a few seconds she looked up into his eyes. His big brown sultry eyes then smacked him square in the face harder than she did before.

"Why are you saying this shit now? Now, of all times you could've said this shit, you choose now?" Red questioned.

"I'm sorry. I'm just not good at putting my feelings out there and shit. Not unless I'm really passionate about some shit." Skid expressed wholeheartedly. "I need you girl."

Red was taken aback by his abundance of love and show of respect for her. She never knew he felt this way about anything let alone anyone seeing as though he had never shown any emotion whatsoever. He was not her ideal candidate for a man. Skid was twenty years her senior and she was not into men that much older than her. He also had a lot of facial and seemingly visible through his white tank top body hair, which she was not a fan of either. Not to mention that he sweated like a slave in the Kentucky sun every time he neared her.

She pulled him in standing on her tippy toes to kiss him. Her tongue rolled around his in a fighting motion but it felt so good. It was if he was tonguing ice cream making sure not one drop fell to the ground. This kiss was even steamier than the one before as she pulled him in tighter while he grabbed a handful of her juicy backside. He moaned heavily amorously feeling his manhood grow desiring every inch of her.

"What are we going to tell Messiah?" She whispered pulling away for a brief second out of breath.

"Why do we need to tell him anything?" Skid wheezed.

Red smiled and continued kissing him using her foot to close the door. Her body was small enough to jump onto his large one and wrap her legs around his waist. His muscles bulged and his veins pulsated as caressed his skin becoming more acquainted with every nook and cranny. She wanted to feel him on a deeper level just as he had. She wanted to love him; giving him the same love he had given her without fail. She had to admit that even though she was not in love with him she did feel something for him. He made her feel brand new like the morning after midnight's rain.

Skid backed his steps up to the sofa in the corner and sat down smoothly so as not to mess up their flow. He massaged her back gripping the small of her back and pulling her close to his chest while she gyrated on him. Her pussy was still throbbing from the flop before with Messiah so she was nice and ripe for the sticking. His burly fingers lifted her t-shirt above his head and flung it on the floor like it was a tiny rubber band unveiling her voluptuous cups as they fell perfectly in front of her. Skid enveloped her erect nipples with his full lips.

"Ahh, baby." Red squealed as he sexually nibbled on her tits.

Red stuck her hand in her jeans fingering her clit rapidly and coupled with Skid's sucking and biting on her tits sent her body into overdrive. She grabbed the back of her head pulling him in closer and closer until he was drowning in tits, but he didn't care. He didn't need to breathe or see just as long as he was in her embrace.

"Fuck me baby." Red exclaimed dismounting him to relieve her waist of her jeans.

Skid rushed to quickly remove his clothes as well looking up to catch a glimpse of her impeccably browned skin. He nearly melted into goop from staring at her temple. She hadn't desecrated it with tattoos and it didn't have any visible war wounds that he cared to pay attention to. For a moment he wondered how could anyone be so cruel to abuse or deface such a special and invaluable work of art.

"Why are you looking at me like that?" Red giggled as she turned to give him a full three sixty view.

"You are just so damn beautiful." His breath was taken away.

"You say the sweetest thing. I knew there was a person under that hard outer shell."

They laughed as he crawled over to her planting tiny pecks on her belly working his way down to V shaped opening. Her legs were together but her clean shaved skin was calling his name.

"Mmmm." He moaned as he engulfed the top skin just above her opening.

"You like that baby?" Red huffed.

"Mmmhmm."

"Well if you like that then you're gonna love this." Red smirked as she kneeled all the way laying her body flat on the floor.

She grabbed his piece finding it already erect and waiting on her. She was amazed by it's girth wanting it like she wanted a bag of money. Her small hand was almost too small to hold it in just one. Her pussy pulsated longing for it to be inside of her and hoping he was way better than the disgrace she had experienced a few hours ago. Red went in for the kill placing his junk in her mouth going all the way down on it like a Bona fide pro and coming up sucking hard enough to suck his seeds right out of him. Skid loved it rough and loved the way her warm mouth felt around his gigantic dick.

"Wait. Mmmm. What are you doing?" He asked trying not to give in to her advances.

"What does it look like I'm doing baby?" Red said coming up for air then going back down to work.

"Naw." Skid hesitated. "Naw. This ain't about me baby. This is about you and my need to feed."

"Huh?" Red laughed feeling like that must have been some old school saying from back in his day.

Skid picked her up by her small frame and carried her like she was as light as a feather over to the island counter just before the kitchen. Red loved the way her manhandled her without struggle or question. She loved the way he took charge like a man should making her want to believe in everything about him. He gradually pushed her back onto the counter laying her down and arching her legs up to her chest spreading her eagle.

"Now my question to you is, do you like this?" Skid smiled as he spread her lips apart with his fingertips and set his tongue on top of her pearl.

"Ahh!" Red moaned as Skid teased and tickled her pearl to no end. "That shit feels so fucking good. Don't stop!"

Skid shook his head. He would never stop not if he could help it. He licked and sucked simultaneously making sure not to waste one drop of her wanting her to cum more and more in his mouth. With two of his large fingers he stuck them slowly inside of her then continued to lick and suck as her legs trembled in ecstasy. She ran her fingers up and down her body before landing them on the back of his head pressing down hard.

She could feel the tension building up inside of her and her temperature along with her clit ready to explode. Skid shook his head copiously feeling her pearl grow in his mouth knowing her time was coming. She had exploded in increments already but it was time for the big bang. The orgasm to complete all orgasms was about to shoot out of her and neither of them could wait. Red pinched each of her nipples concurrently increasing her pleasure level to one hundred percent.

"Shit. I'm gonna cum baby! Make me cum hard!" Red breathed loudly spreading her legs as far as she could get them helping him plant his face deeper.

Skid moved his fingers in and out of her opening as fast as he could fucking her nicely as he pleasured her pearl with his tongue to no end. He was not even tired and could actually go all night if she had let him. He reached his free hand up to her tits caressing them softly but was interrupted by Red's hand interlocking her fingers with his. It was the first time he had ever

felt true unconditional love from someone. Though the
gesture was small it showed him that she cared for him
despite their differences, short time frame of his
proclamation of love and ages. She was giving him a
sense of intimacy.

"Argh! Ah, ah, ah!" Red yelled smiling that she
had finally gotten off in the best way possible. "Thank
you, thank you, thank you!"

Skid laughed. "You ain't gotta thank me baby.
I'll do that shit every night all night if you want me to."

Skid leaned back down flicking the tip of his
tongue on her pearl once more thirsty for more of her
taste in his mouth. She didn't want to fight it but that
part of her longings was fulfilled for now. It was time
quench her yearning for some beef in between her tight
little walls.

"Hey baby. Come on up here and show me what
that big ass dick feels like." She purred.

"Yes, ma'am. Whatever you say." He panted.

He picked her up tonguing her all the way to the
sofa releasing her to sit effortlessly. She immediately
got up from the sofa and waited for him to take the
note to sit down. Even though he said it was all about
her, she couldn't bring herself to just lay on her back
traditionally when he had so eloquently given her the
best head she had been given in years. He took his cue
sitting down on the sofa allowing her to mount him like
he was a strong stallion.

She slid down on his shaft like butter, slow but
easy. Her tight youthful pussy immersed him securely
downing him in one gulp. Red released a sexy little
whimper but she was determined to be a big girl and
take his massive sized dick all the way in. Skid loved
every minute of it leaning his head back on the sofa

ready to relax and enjoy. She bounced up and down swiftly, rolling her hips allowing him to dig inside of her pressuring her to climax. Her ass cheeks bounced hard giving his legs a good beating on the way down. He grabbed them, squeezing tightly as his warmth rose, being a sucker for a fat ass.

"Ahh, shit! Mmm, yeah!" Red screamed.

"Take this dick baby! You like that, huh? You like this dick?" Skid tauntingly asked as he forcefully pushed her cheeks down on his dick harder and harder.

"Yes baby! Hell yes!"

"Do you love me baby? I wanna hear you say it." Skid could feel his climax approaching but he was determined to hold it back. "Say it!"

Red paused for a moment uncertain as to if she should answer the question or not. Unsure of what to say she filled the air with her loud screeching and moaning. His dick felt so good in fact, that she was already on her third orgasm since mounting the oversized Johnson. Skid leaned forward still gripping her ass and flicked his tongue around her nipples sending chills of excitement through her. He scooted down planting his feet firmly on the floor the thrust his pelvis into her making her yelp in pain but still pleasure. Her screams became more high pitched with every thrust he made breaking her down slowly as her pussy ejaculated all over him.

"Say it!" He commanded now ejaculating inside of her never thinking twice. "Say it."

"I love you, baby." She exhaled closing her eyes and kissing his neck sweetly.

Chapter 19
Bitch

The next morning, Messiah found himself slipping out from under Alexis and Braze as they lay on the floor holding each other in a warm embrace. Shit went down last night that was never supposed to happen but they were drunk and he was horny. He was a little upset with himself that he was able to perform for them and not for Red, wondering if his dick was trying to tell him that he really was not as in love with Red as he thought he was.

He jumped in the shower scrubbing his balls more than twice and when he was done he brushed his teeth for a full thirty minutes. It was amazing that with all the commotion in the room that night, MJ only woke up once. He couldn't wait until his little man woke up so he could snuggle him to death. When he emerged from the bathroom he headed to the master bedroom to dress in one of his suits as usual but today he would forgo the tie to keep it a bit casual. He threw on a baby blue short sleeve button down, black slacks and matching blazer. Sliding into his favorite pair of Steve Madden's, he checked hisself out in the mirror one last time to make sure he was tight then headed back to the room to kiss his soon before he left for the day.

The room was still silent when he pushed the door open. Looking around he noticed that everybody was gone the room was empty. He looked around confused for a minute then headed down to the kitchen to see if they were down there. The kitchen was alive with laughter and the smell of scrambled cheese eggs and fried bacon. MJ was sitting on a beanbag that Alexis had found for him in Messiah's rec room. The scene was rather weird to him even though the events from the night before should have dissipated any feelings of that.

"Hey baby. You want some breakfast?" Alexis smiled scraping some eggs from a skillet that Braze handed her.

"You cooking?" Messiah asked with uncertainty in his voice.

"Well Braze is helping me."

"Oh. Well, naw I'm good. I gotta run anyway. But it looks great." Messiah declared as he reached down to pick up his son cooing in his face.

"Ugh. Are we going to talk about the elephant in the room?" Braze grilled.

"Let me start." Alexis announced quickly. "Braze and I were talking and she basically apologized for lying to me and told me the truth."

"So…you two are friends?" Messiah queried ambiguously.

"It's not that simple." Braze answered.

"No, not really. But we are cordial to each other at this point and this is your son so —" Alexis paused.

"So we were thinking that we could grow to like each other, maybe even love each other."

The two women looked at each other hugged each other's side with one arm and tossing a smile each way. For a split second, the scene in the kitchen looked like one big happy family. The thoughts running through Messiah's head were not only sexual in nature but also happy as well. He started to believe that he might be able to pull this off as long as he would be able to convince Alexis to be cool about it once she got her memory back. It was a long shit but he was willing to try it thinking how much fun it would be to have two women in his house with no beef and be able to have them anytime he wanted.

"And y'all would be cool with that? I could have you or you whenever I wanted with no drama or together if I wanted?" Messiah attempted to clarify.

"Yep."

"Yeah, pretty much."

The women laughed.

"Damn! Well alright!" Messiah laughed and as soon as he kissed his son and set him back down on the beanbag he realized he was forgetting one small thing. Red. "Alright y'all I gotta go. I'll holla at y'all later."

"Um." Alexis cleared her throat. "Can we get a goodbye kiss?"

Braze liked that idea but she wanted to ensure that she got her kiss first. She knew it would be like this every single day for the rest of her life or until she could get Alexis' ass out of the picture. No matter what they did or how it went down she was going to be first. Period. Alexis was standing closer to Messiah and naturally walked around the counter headed for the first goodbye kiss. Just as she was nearing him to wrap her arms around his neck, Braze hurriedly walked to beat her to the chase hopping over her son and purposely tripping Alexis in the process.

Alexis fell on her butt hard and thumping the back of her head on the counter even harder. Braze tried to ignore it by slamming her kiss on Messiah smiling as if she had done no wrong. MJ began crying at the top of her lungs as Braze suddenly felt her waist being pushed away. Messiah snapped his fingers silently ordering her to handle the baby while he moved over to help Alexis off the floor.

"You okay?" He asked side eyeing Braze.

"My fucking head is pounding." Alexis replied with pain on her face.

"Maybe you should go upstairs and lay down."

"Yeah thanks, Messiah. When I want your advice I'll ask for it alright."

The room grew silent as everyone looked up into Alexis' eyes. She didn't know what the hell they were staring at but she did know that it was slowly pissing her off. Her anger rose with every second and the minute sounds of the kitchen were rattling the headache in her skull. She looked around the room at the breakfast scattered on the counter and the whining baby being rocked and breast fed by Braze. Then she turned her attention back to Messiah and suddenly remembered everything from before the accident and also everything after leading up to this point. The thing that mostly stood out to her was the fact that Messiah was moving forward with the divorce she was forbidding from happening.

"Why are you snapping on me?" Messiah asked hesitantly.

Alexis knew that in order to get through this with everything she wanted and more she would have to continue to play this little game. "Oh! Oh, yes baby I'm fine. I'm sorry I was just a little dazed there."

"Uh...do you remember anything?" Braze asked Alexis while she was staring at Messiah curiously.

"What? Oh God no. I'm still drawing a blank. Sorry to burst your bubble guys. But that was one hard fall though, huh?" Alexis said walking over to Messiah stretching her tongue into his mouth like a porn star pro. "I guess I'd better be more careful, huh, Braze?

Alexis wiped her lips squinting her eyes at Braze and MJ. She sucked her lips as she grabbed the breakfast dishes and tossed the uneaten food into the garbage disposal. Braze was livid inside having worked on that breakfast too damn hard for her to waste it all like that, not to mention she was mega hungry right then.

"Alright ladies play nice. I'm gone." Messiah stated as he kissed his son once more and darted out the door.

"I made that breakfast because I was hungry. You don't have to eat it if you don't want to. I'll clean up the mess." Braze protested as she lowered her sleeping full son back down on the beanbag.

"I can't stand to see my kitchen in clutter." Alexis' voice was no longer inviting in fact it was cold.

Braze walked over trying to get a good look at her face suspecting that something was up with her. She didn't seem like the pleasant person she was yesterday. For the first time since she devised her evil plan to live under one roof with Messiah and his wife it finally dawned on her that she just might be asked to leave one day too soon.

"You did get your memory back, didn't you? Just now, right then?" Braze asked crossing her arms.

"What's it to you? As long as you get a free fucking place to stay that's all you care about right?" Alexis yowled as she scrubbed the same spot of the counter for ten minutes straight. "I mean what else could you want? You already have my husband's baby. Let me guess, you want him too right?"

Braze was silent staring at the sun shining through the window. Alexis turned to see the expression on her face and coupled with the silence she knew exactly what Braze's intentions were. It would have pissed her off if it weren't for one thing. She had the ring and was determined to keep it. There was not a chance in hell that she would relinquish it to her just because she had a bald headed baby whom she claimed was his.

"You know, you're not the only one he's brought up in here talking about 'this my baby's momma'."

"What?"

"Yeah…and then we'd do a blood test and find out that bitch was lying through her teeth just so she could get some money. So we kicked her bum ass out on the street." Alexis laughed as she turned back around resuming her cleaning.

"Is that what you wanna do to me?"

"No. At least not yet anyway. You're gonna help me save my marriage and while you're doing that we're gonna get this little baby here a small test, if you know what I mean."

"Help your marriage? That's not what I came here for."

"I know. You, like all the rest of the hoes, figure you can take my place. You all figure you can be me and steal my life and my man and live happily ever after being the better woman for him. But what you bitches don't really don't know is even if he got the chance to leave me, it would only be a matter of time before he did the same shit to you."

"Messiah's been playing all of us for years."

"Oh, don't trip." Alexis said pouring herself a glass of Merlot. "It was mostly my fault for not trying to fix my marriage in the beginning. Instead I just went out and fucked his brother...and whoever else wanted to slide up in my shit."

"I think we're just misunderstood women who happen to be in love with the same man. And if you lay off the booze a little and appreciate what you have, maybe we could be a happy family. You..." Braze walked over taking her drink from her hand and pulling her neck down to her short level then sucking passionately. "me, Messiah and our son."

"Our son? I don't even like kids." Alexis tried to fight her but her tongue felt so warm and tantalizing on her neck.

"You'll learn." Braze replied as she carefully removed her silk purple nighty from her body.

It fell naturally to the floor unveiling her voluptuous tall golden skinned body. It was beautiful in every way. Braze smiled admiring her, running her fingertips from her V like opening and up to her nipples then placed on of the gently on her lips. She Eskimo kissed her nipples taunting them to become erect and making Alexis' pussy dripping wet at the same time. Braze squatted down on her knees placing her tongue on the very outskirts of her pussy pressing against it firmly.

She licked from the opening just barely touching her protruding clit and working her way all the way up to her tits where she sucked them for two seconds each. Alexis kept her hands down to her side in total shock that a woman was treating her this way and she liked it. Her face was pulled into Braze's by her hands for a brief tongue wrestling match.

"And you'll learn to love me too, bitch. Cause like it or not, I ain't going nowhere. Me and my son are here to stay. So you either get with the program or you get left behind. I can and will destroy you boo. But I'd rather lick your pussy 'til its dry." Braze walked over to the beanbag swooping up MJ in one swift motion. "You make the call."

Braze left the room and Alexis finally released the breath she was holding when Braze walked away from her. She just knew that she was going to get her pussy licked like none other right then. It was amazing that a woman could touch her, lick her, or make her feel so sexy and sensual. It intrigued her to no end. She yearned for more like a crack head yearned for his next fix. Breathing heavily, biting her lip and feeling like she was going to cum on herself, her legs left her nighty on the kitchen floor. Then she disabled her mind allowing her pussy to lead her upstairs.

Chapter 20
Exposed

Red woke up on the sofa alone. Her naked body was covered in a white sheet she recognized as being one of those from her linen closet. Considering the night's events, to her surprise, she was completely well rested. There was only one person who she could contribute to that and that was Skid. She immediately rose forgetting about covering herself to find out where he was. The apartment was silent. Her thoughts ran rampant figuring he only used her for sex. All of that bullshit he said was only to fulfill his own sick needs.

Rejection, heartbreak, and being used were feelings she knew all to well. Red knew it would be a long shot to find someone who was different from all the other assholes she had encountered in her lifetime. She was now faced with the issue of if Skid would run off and tell Messiah that he banged her and fuck up her chances with him too.

With her head hung mighty low she headed towards the back hoping to finally get a nice hot shower in with no interruptions. As she neared the bathroom she peeked over into her bedroom at the minuscule coagulated blood pattered on the wall and realized the majority of the mess was missing.

"Good morning." Skid said emerging from behind the door.

"AH!" Red jumped back, holding her chest and startled by his presence. "You scared the shit out of me."

"Why'd I scare you? You knew I was here...right?"

"Well...I didn't see you and it was so quiet in here I just thought—"

"You thought I left you?" Skid inquired. "I see we've got some more learning to do about each other. I would never do you like that."

"Sorry." Red apologized biting her bottom lip playfully.

"I only left your side to clean the room before it settled in. You sleeping on my body made it the best night of my life. I promise to never let you wake up alone again. Okay?" Skid explained giving her lips a tender peck.

"Okay."

"Great. Now saunter that sexy ass on in the kitchen and cook a nigga somethin' to eat." Skid laughed as he friskily smacked her on the ass.

"Uh, there's just one problem with that babe. I don't have any food here."

The two of them laughed. They were hardly ever home, which meant they ate out more often than not. He pulled her in for a long tongue lashing then kissed her forehead slowly and tenderly.

"Then I guess we'd better hit an Ihop or something. Get dressed. I'm almost done here." Skid said as he walked over to scrub the small remaining amount of blood of the wall. "That'll be cool anyway, though. I need to talk to you about something."

"Talk about what?" Red asked as she slipped on a pair of jeans and pink laced bra with matching tank top.

"Well its not some shit that should be taken lightly and I need to sit and explain it."

"Skid, don't sugar coat shit for me and beat around the bush now. After all this and you gonna pussy foot me?"

He sighed harshly not wanting to deal with the issue right then but because time was of the essence he knew he would have. It was a conversation that might indeed fuck up their beautiful night and amorous morning. Skid took the rubber gloves off his hands and tossed them on the floor then walked over to her taking her by the hand and leading her into the living room. He extended his hand for her to sit down while he stood pacing trying to get his thoughts together before he spoke.

"Alright, I need you to help me out with something. But I need to know that when I ask you to do this you will be all in this for me." Skid said bringing his pacing to a halt.

"Oh my God. You're not going to ask me to marry you are you? I mean that sounds nice and shit but damn Skid I'm just getting used to us as a freakin' couple. I love you and I can be in love with you deeply, I see it, but marriage." Red hyperventilated.

"Huh? Girl you trippin'. I ain't thinkin' about that shit right now. Don't twist it, I would marry you. But no that's not what this is about."

"Then what is this about?" Red questioned as she stood caressing his broad chest.

He quickly grabbed her hands pushing her away from him so he could think clearly on what needed to be said. Skid rubbed his head roughly then looked back down at her big gorgeous brown eyes and wondered how he could ever ask her to do his bidding for him. Just as he was about to speak there was a mild knock on the door. He signaled for her to keep silent while he slowly moved over to check the peephole to see whom the visitor was. His heart dropped when he saw the figure standing outside the door immediately recognizing him. Before he opened the door he checked for his piece making sure it was securely placed behind his back.

"Do you love me?" Skid whispered as he turned to Red.

"Of course I do." Red replied a bit bewildered as to why he was asking this with his hand on the doorknob.

"Then tell him." He said as he opened the door.

Red watched as Messiah walked in the door. She gasped and her heart sunk to the pits of her stomach. She stood and cut her eyes from one man to the other back and forth wondering what kind of shit Skid had pulled on her. Her lips were stuck open and her palms were sweaty like she had just finished working out at the gym.

"Hey, uh, hey y'all." Messiah said as he looked around the room noticing a few things in disarray and solemn looks on their faces. "Who died?"

"Um…" Red mumbled.

"We had a little problem here last night but it was handled." Skid interrupted eyeing her from across the room.

"Oh. Okay then. So, then we don't have a problem. Skid could you give us some time alone. I need to holla at her real quick."

"No."

"What? Nigga what the fuck you mean no?"

"No." Skid repeated. "Red has something she wants to say to you."

Red stared back at him clenching her hands in front of her. She really didn't want to say anything to Messiah but everything that she had seen and heard last night came rushing back to her. She stared into Messiah's eyes knowing that he was just about to lie to her about whatever and knew she had no reason to stand for the shit anymore. Her eyes cut back to Skid smiling at him as he winked at her.

"Messiah, we are done. Skid is my man now and you need to deal with that." She announced with confidence.

"Huh? When the fuck this happen?" Messiah had gone from zero to fifty in a matter of seconds. "You been fucking him all this time?"

"No! No, we actually just got together." She explained.

"Oh yeah. When?"

"Last night."

Messiah busted out laughing his ass off. He felt like it was all a joke what she was telling him and if it wasn't a joke there was no way she could call this dude her man when they had only been together for less than twenty-four hours. After he got a good laugh in he turned to Skid and shook his head at how disloyal he had been to him. Out of everyone who had played him he was hurt to find out that Skid was one of those self-serving back stabbing motherfuckas too.

"So this what you do, huh? I thought you was my man. A hundred grand." Messiah uttered.

"Ay, maybe if you wasn't so busy chasin' hoes that wasn't shit than maybe you could've had her. I'm gonna show her what a real man does." Skid sucked his teeth unscathed by Messiah's attempt to guilt him.

"Is that right?"

"That's right, Meech. But I'm glad you're here, you see cause my woman is the least of your problems." Skid warned.

"Wait, Skid. Is this what you wanted to talk to me about?" Red asked not wanting a fight to break out over her.

"Babe, your guy here hasn't been paying his debts and now his debtor wants to collect. That's why the Candy Shop hasn't been prospering like it used to and it's also the reason why most of his soldiers went rogue. He stopped upping that money like he did in the beginning."

"What? You're broke?" Red said shaking her head. "And my rape could've been avoided if you had've just paid your fucking men too, huh?"

"Man, Zadie set you up, man. Don't blame that shit on me!" Messiah snapped. "Fuck that! I'm the one who sent the order up to go look for you. I'm the one!"

"Yeah while you were in the hospital with your wife." Skid added.

"Ugh! The very wife that you were sleeping with last night with your little fuck toy, Braze." Red continued.

"What? How do you—" Messiah paused.

"You didn't think I knew about that, baby? Why wouldn't I? I'm not as stupid as I look Messiah?"

Messiah looked around the room feeling like he had been set up royally. He started kicking hisself in the ass figuratively feeling like for this kind of drama he could have stayed at home. It slowly began to dawn on him that the only way she could know about last night was if someone tipped her off or if someone who was there sent her proof. It plagued his mind but he knew there was nothing he could do about it now.

"Tell her Meech. Tell her how you had been playing her since the beginning. That's why you never told her about Alexis. You figured you could do to her what you did to Braze and have your cake and eat it too." Skid said as he gazed into her eyes.

"Man this is really some bitch shit, you know that? You did all this for what? For some pussy? You couldn't get pussy on your own so you had to lie to get huh?" Messiah turned walking towards Red reaching out to grab her arm. "Baby, you gonna believe this nigga over me?"

"Yeah. I think I am." She said as she snatched away from his touch.

Skid turned around and took out his Iphone checking for any missed calls before anyone could notice. There were a ton of them. He stuffed it back into his pocket quickly then walked over to Red taking the midsized black gun from behind his back and handed it to her. He stood behind her hovering over her like a dark cloud holding her hands around the gun.

"What's this for?" She asked.

"I want you to make sure this nigga don't go nowhere. I'm going to go make a phone call." Skid kissed her cheek then eyed Messiah as he headed back towards the bedroom and closed the door.

"So this is what we've come to, Red? I thought we were better than that." Messiah barked.

"I'm sorry. I can't let you go."

"Do you even know why you can't let me go? This nigga got you runnin' shit for him and you don't even know why. You let this nigga fuck you stupid."

"Excuse me? First of all its none of your business what he did to me and second of all if he did fuck me stupid you better believe it was way better than the three seconds of fun you shot in my mouth."

"Bitch! I treated you like a fucking queen and you repay me like this?" Messiah's voiced raised six octaves above normal as he began to panic wanting out of the apartment. "I'm out! You can't hold me here."

"After all I've gone through because of you, you would fix your lips to call me a bitch?" Red smirked. "Messiah, I'm warning you. If you move I'm gonna blow your fucking head off."

"You ain't got the balls to shoot me. I know don't."

"Then you don't know me very well." She retorted raising the gun up pointing right in between his eyes. "You already know I'm a beast for it. Ask your girl Zadie."

"Redina—"

"You know I used to think you were the man of the decade. You were so suave and distinguished. But now I see your nothing but a pathetic loser who treats women like toilet paper."

"You don't know what you're talking about. I did love you Red."

"Yes but you loved her more huh?" Red shook her head forcing herself to fight back tears. "Just like you loved her last night."

"Redina, you don't understand. My intentions were to put both of those hoes out of my life. I only wanted you, but then..." Messiah paused as he remembered what was told to him this morning.

Chapter 21
"Loaded, baby."—Red

Messiah was excited just this morning to have two women vying for his love and attention. It was intriguing to him that he held that kind of power over them. But he knew it would all come at a cost and that cost would be Red's heart. He truly did love her deep down inside but the fact of the matter was he had no control over the women in his life. In that area, he was the weakest.

"But then what, Messiah?"

"Look," Messiah sighed. "I'm sorry alright. I never meant to hurt you and I surely didn't want you to end up in the arms of this clown."

"He treats me like a fucking queen. He worships me."

"Shit I worshipped you. But I guess that don't mean shit huh?" Messiah laughed.

"Naw, it used to mean something but you can't keep bitches off you and your dick in your pants. See what you fail to realize is that Skid helped me open my eyes. He didn't have to tell me much about you that I didn't figure out for myself." Red snapped pacing the room. "You're a fucking liar. Just admit it."

"I ain't admitting shit cause I did love you. That nigga just mad cause I never promoted his ass and now he's tryin' to be me."

"You need to start taking responsibility for your own shit. I don't know exactly what's going on but I do know whatever it is you brought it on yourself." Red said raising her gun back up to his face.

"Bitch!" Messiah exploded as he rushed towards her trying to get at the gun.

Red wrestled him as the fell back on the sofa. She locked her legs around his waist and held her arm up as far away from him as she possibly could. Messiah wasn't even focusing on getting the gun just then figuring he could use all of his strength to squeeze the life out of her and force her to hand it over. She looked down trying to figure out a way to bite his face but he was too far down on her body for her mouth to reach. They struggled a great deal before Messiah finally attempted to try and take the gun from her hand.

"I will shoot you motherfucka! I will! Get off me!" Red screamed.

"If you wanted to do it you would've done it by now." Messiah said as he bit down on her tit taking in a large chunk.

Red released an unimaginable squeal as she used her feet trying to kick him off of her but it was no use. His body was so heavy and he just kept scaling up her like he was King Kong and she was the Empire State building. Skid exited the room running up to the struggle and bopped Messiah on the back of the head forcing him to roll off of her and onto the floor. Messiah clenched his head riddled with headache as he clung to the side of the sofa trying to bring hisself to his feet.

"Hey baby. You alright?" Skid asked helping Red up off the sofa.

"Yeah, I'm fine." She side eyed. "Took you long enough though."

"I'm sorry babe. I had to handle some business. It won't happen again." Skid assured her, his voice stern and firm.

"I hope you weren't back there talking to some b—"

"Ah, don't do that. You feel me better than that. I know you do. Don't let this nigga's corruption come in and fuck your mind up. You know me." Skid said hawking her down.

"Okay." Red smiled as she turned to kick Messiah back down on the floor. "You never cared about me. Fucking liar."

"Shit, this proves you don't care about me." He snapped.

"Shut up. She doesn't need to care about you no more with yo' punk ass." Skid snapped back as phone sounded off. "Hello. Yeah, here I come."

Skid kissed Red's forehead and gave her the wait notion as he headed out of the front door. Red promised herself she wouldn't be caught off guard again if Messiah tried any funny business. She planted her feet firmly on the ground then watched him like she was glued to a television unable to blink or take her eyes off of him. He simply rolled over onto his back and lay there staring up at the ceiling.

"So how much did they offer you?" He asked breathing heavily.

"What? I don't know what you're talking about."

"The niggas up north, how much, how much?"

"I don't know what the fuck you're talking about!" Red shouted having her fill of Messiah and his bullshit and wondering where the hell Skid was.

"Yeah he's in here."

Red heard Skid say from the other side of the door. As the door flung open, two men dressed in khaki knee length shorts and colorful Hawaiian shirts came inside before him. They looked like something fresh out of a Miami Vice episode with their protruding beer bellies and their slicked back hair. These men were not of African decent but their skin was as bronze as hers was. She knew that these guys were not from around there no matter how badly they tried to fit in.

"Meech get yo bitch ass up. You got company." Skid said kicking his feet.

"Ah, hello gentlemen. Crazy us meeting like this don't ya think?" Messiah laughed as he struggled to sit up, still dazed from the blow to his head.

"Get your ass up, Meech. We're done playing this game, with you now." One of the obese men commanded. "Where's our fucking money, coon?"

"Yeah. Where's their fucking money, Meech?" Skid cosigned as Haggley came walking in the door with a large black briefcase in hand.

"Messiah. You look alive and well, but that'll soon change. How ya doin'?" Haggley laughed as he walked in handing Skid the case.

Skid eagerly grabbed the case from his hands then moved over to the island setting it up there. He clicked the latches on it and as the top flew open his eyes grew wider than the Sahara Desert. All of his wildest dreams could be fulfilled with the contents of this simple ordinary worker's briefcase. There was more green in the case than there was on a beautifully maintained golf course.

"Skid, you are dismissed." Haggley said waving his hands as if he were a common peasant.

"Wait, what's going on here?" Red asked dropping her weapon down to her side.

"Don't ask questions you don't need the answers to, babe. Com' on' let's leave these gentlemen to their job." Skid said wrapping his arm around her torso and escorting her out the door.

"Skid I don't feel right about this. If they gon' rough him up that's one thing but he's got a baby and shit he needs to live for."

"Why do you care so much? You still love him, don't you?" Skid said as he walked over the grass headed for his truck.

"Why do you hate him so much? At one point in time he was your friend. Yeah he's bogus as hell for some shit he does but that doesn't make him a bad person." Red replied, feeling sorry for Messiah.

She couldn't deny that she was still in love with him even though she knew he was toxic for her. Her feelings wouldn't get in the way of what was morally right. Messiah was only heartbroken after all that she had left him and slept with Skid but she knew he realized that he had hurt her too. Red stood outside the truck as he tossed the case inside the truck then rotated to her.

"What the fuck, Red? I thought we had something girl."

"We do." She said walking up to his chest caressing it devotedly. "But I don't want our love to be tainted. Not like this."

Skid looked into her eyes knowing that no matter what she said she was only doing this because she was still in love with him. It killed him deep inside to think about that even though he buried the fact down inside of his heart. He stared amorously in her eyes feeling like she would never be able to stop thinking about Messiah and she would never forgive him if he were dead. She would lie to his face about her feelings because it would be a constant reminder of her love for him.

"What is it gonna take for you to love me like I love you?" Skid asked standing toe-to-toe with her and breathing down her neck.

The sounds of a pain punched through the walls of Red's apartment rattling their ears like bass drums. Red closed her eyes then reopened them hoping that they would have mercy on Messiah's soul. He was not a bad man in her eyes, just one that made bad decisions. She looked deep into Skid's eyes, her feelings growing stronger for him by the second, her bottom lip taking a beating from her teeth as she prepared to answer him truthfully.

"Nothing. I love you already. I promise you that no matter what happens here, I will never speak of him after this day."

"But will you think of him?" Skid asked worriedly.

"Never. I wanna love you and you only." Red was sure to keep her eyes firmly on his and nothing else so he could tell she was real. "That's my word."

"Shit." Skid shook his head breaking free from their gaze.

He went back into the car looking up under the seat yanking hard then slammed the door hard. In front of Red, he tossed his second thoughts out the window feeling the adrenaline rush through his veins. It seemed like the wrong place and time for her pussy to get wet but she had to admit seeing him in killa mode turned her on to the max.

"You still got that piece?" Skid asked cocking his back.

"Loaded, baby."

"Aight stay low and stay behind me." He kissed her lips hard. "I'm trustin' you to have my back."

"Always."

They headed back towards the apartment noticing that the men did not bother to close the door all the way. The closer they got to the door the more silently they crept listening in as the men taunted and beat Messiah almost to a bloody pulp. Skid looked back at Red, winking his eye at her then rushed the door blasting strategically as if he was part of the Black Ops. Red followed close behind him blasting the two obese men instantaneously without stopping, drilling hole after hole into their stout chests. She was a beast with the steel making sure she put down whoever got in her path. Haggley ran to the back room busting back at Skid the whole way. Red looked at Messiah nearly dead in a pool of his own blood reaching up his hand to her. She felt sorry for him looking down onto his badly bruised and beaten face but ran to the back of the room as guns shots sounded off like multiple fireworks.

"Skid!" Red busted open the bedroom door raising the gun up.

Haggley stood there holding the gun up to Skid's head as he lay on the floor seemingly wounded. The crooked cop laughed as he backed up towards the window limping and in pain from the gun shot wounds to his leg and shoulder.

"Shoot him baby!" Skid bellowed in agony.

"Yeah shoot me so I can shoot him." Haggley laughed sinisterly with blood seeping out from the right side of his body. "Nobody gets hurt, Skid. We can all go home. Just call off your bitch."

"My name is not bitch!" Boom! Boom! Boom! "It's Redina motherfucka!"

She ran over to check the severity of Skid's wounds. "Baby, are you okay?"

"Yeah, yeah. I'll be cool. It's just my arm."

Red looked concerned hoping that he would not bleed out before she could get him to some help. A gunshot wound was nothing to play with but he was acting like it was a simple walk in the park. She helped him to his feet ready to hop in the car and leave the immense blood bath behind. They knew with all the commotion someone had triggered the cops and they wouldn't be too far away from the scene. In the living room, Messiah was still struggling to get up so he could flee the scene himself.

"Shit, could y'all help a nigga out?" Messiah asked leaning on the sofa ledge trying to pull himself up.

"A nigga, huh?" Red leered. "Naw, I think we've helped you out enough."

Messiah finally brought hisself to his feet, shaking and dazed. He stumbled towards the door leaving his bloody handprints all on the wall and door as he sprinted out. He looked back at them as they exited the apartment closing the door behind them. The look on his face was one to haunt even the hardest of criminals as he jumped in his truck and swerved off into the ongoing traffic.

Skid shook his head knowing that Messiah was a bitch ass nigga inside and out. He always looked for someone to help him out and he always looked for a shoulder to lean on. He was a coward who could never stand on his own two feet and if it weren't for Red he would have left that nigga in that apartment with them niggas, period. The Italians were nothing to fuck with and knew it was only a matter of time before someone found out what had happened and came looking for Messiah again. The thought ran through both of their minds as they walked to the truck. Sooner or later Messiah would have to answer to the Made Man and quite possibly if he was a snitch like that, so would they.

"Get in. I'm driving." Skid said nodding his head towards the other side of the truck.

"Fool, how you gon' drive with that bad arm?"

"Girl, just get yo' ass in the car."

She did as she was told, not wanting to rile him up in his current state. They drove off surprisingly not hearing one siren coming towards the complex. On the road, Skid used his hand to assess the wound realizing that it might have been more critical than he originally thought. Red saw him struggling with the wheel, looking up at his face.

"Babe we gotta get you to a hospital fast." She demanded scared for his well being.

"I know…I'm headed there now." Skid replied groggily. "But I'm cool though. Don't trip. It just stings like hell, that's all."

"Well, what about the Candy Shop?" Red asked.

"Woman, fuck that shop. I'll get you your own business where you won't ever have to lift a finger, ya heard? That shop was dead a long time ago, right along with ya boy." Skid paused. "I hope you know he still has a bounty, Red. He won't last long."

"Hmm. His blood isn't on our hands after this." She noted hesitantly. "So do you think they'll hunt us down?"

"It don't matter…if they come." Skid spoke deviously. "We'll be ready for them."

"Motherfuckin' right baby." Red grimaced worriedly looking over noticing that his condition was worsening. "Gotta get to this hospital."

STAY UP TO DATE ON THE LATEST GOING ON

WITH NICETY!

FOLLOW ME:

@NICETYCOUTURE

LIKE ME ON FACEBOOK:

.com/NICETYCOUTURE

DON'T FORGET TO REVIEW!

#GETFIXATED

#VISUALFIXATION

#TEAMNICETY